A CHRISTMAS MYSTERY

GREEN VALLEY

NOELLE ADAMS

This book is a work of fiction. Names, characters, places, and incidents are the product of the author's imagination or are used fictitiously. Any resemblance to actual events, locales, or persons, living or dead, is coincidental.

Copyright © 2024 by Noelle Adams. All rights reserved, including the right to reproduce, distribute, or transmit in any form or by any means.

1

I wake up at 7:21 in the morning two Thursdays before Christmas.

For the past two years, I haven't set my alarm, but I've gradually begun going to bed earlier, so I'm naturally waking up earlier too. Starting my mornings between seven and eight always feels best, and I'm pleased when I check the time on the wooden clock carved with birds on the wall across from my bed.

It's my 753rd morning waking up alone after Chris, my fiancé, died in a car accident three weeks before our wedding date. For the first year, I always woke up with a heavy weight in my gut even when I wasn't consciously sad. But that's slowly been changing—lightening—and this morning I feel really good.

I'm back in Green Valley, North Carolina. My hometown. I'll be here through Christmas and New Year's Day, and I'm excited about the next three weeks.

Not about the holidays. All the artificial excitement and festivities don't appeal to me anymore.

And not about encountering a slew of old acquaintances, none of whom know me as the person I am now. They only know me as Chris's girl. Then his fiancée. Maya Alexander. The absent-minded, artsy-crafty one who could never complete projects or even hold a regular job for more than a few months at a time.

But I am excited about seeing Tee, my great-aunt who raised me from the age of seven, and my cousin, Daniela.

I'm also excited about solving the mystery of my secret pen pal who's been sending me messages for almost a year but refuses to identify himself.

The only thing I know for sure is that he's a man and that he lives in Green Valley. He appears to have a history there, so he likely went to school with me.

Green Valley kids tend not to leave town, and if they do leave, they eventually move back. I would still be living there too had I not lost Chris and desperately needed to get away.

So my pen pal is probably a Green Valley local—born and raised and still living in town.

Before I take off again after New Year's, I'm going to find out who he is.

I'm lying in bed, mulling over my plans for the next

three weeks, when Claude climbs the stairs to my bedroom loft, leaps onto the mattress, and walks up my body to peer into my face with his intelligent gold eyes.

Claude is my Bombay cat—sleek and black and eerily clever. He's a dramatic contrast to Ed, my big, fluffy orange tabby who is currently curled up, snoring on the second pillow beside my head.

"I'm getting up," I tell Claude, who is ready for breakfast and disapproves of my sloth. "You don't have to glare at me like that. You can't be *that* hungry."

At the sound of my voice—or maybe at the word "hungry"—Ed lifts his head and squints at me.

"I know. It's breakfast time."

That's enough to motivate even Ed to heft himself onto all four paws. With a sigh, I sit up, taking care not to hit my head on the low slope of the loft's ceiling. I pull on an oversized sweater over my pajamas and then climb down the stairs carefully since they are narrow and built right against the wall.

The small kitchen is under the loft, so the ceiling is low there too. I slice a lemon and add half to a glass of water before going outside to walk as I drink it.

Mid-December in North Carolina is often fairly mild. It's in the high forties this morning, and the sun is starting to rise. It's brisk but not uncomfortable beside the lake. I walk around the campground until I've finished my glass of water, clearing my mind and taking deep breaths in a way I've practiced every morning since Chris died.

Early on, this form of meditation was the only way I could keep myself from crawling back into bed to cry for the rest of the day, but now it mostly helps begin my days with a peaceful, settled heart.

Theo Humphrey would probably call it trendy, empty spiritualism. I was into crystals for a year after college, and Theo always eyed them disapprovingly. He was Chris's best friend ever since kindergarten, and he thought I was too silly and frivolous to be a good match for his friend.

Chris was hardworking and practical, but he never cared that I was different. That I love crafting and thrifting and art and unusual mental health habits and ritual and deep spirituality. Chris loved me for who I am and wanted me to pursue whatever made me happy, but Theo never understood. He still doesn't.

Of all the people in Green Valley I don't want to see over the holidays, Theo is at the top of the list.

I shake the image of his thick, wavy auburn hair and grumpy expression out of my head so that I won't lose my pleasant mood. Then I return to my tiny house to make coffee in the French press.

I bought this tiny house with part of the inheritance and life insurance money I received after Chris's death. It's adorable—only two hundred square feet in a cottage style with a small fold-down deck on the side. What Chris left me has allowed me to travel all over the country in the past two years, towing my house and staying for a few weeks at a time in campgrounds and parks.

Even before losing Chris, I was never really built for a regular nine-to-five job, and for months afterward there was no way I could focus enough to work. So I traveled. I did a lot of praying and meditation and reading and crafting. I disconnected from news and television and all the scrolling on social media I used to rely on for stimulation. I only kept my Instagram account, using it like a journal to post photos and brief reflections on grief and healing and providing my friends and family updates on life traveling in my tiny house.

And slowly more people began to follow me. I didn't consciously work to gain new followers. I barely even noticed the first year as friends would share my posts and new people would like my photos or interact with my meditations or wish me well. But by the second year, my large number of followers changed life for me.

I was able to monetize the account. Brands started contacting me, wanting me to form partnerships. I had to obscure my personal details and specific locations since having such a large number of people knowing exactly who and where I am, traveling as a woman alone, was no longer safe.

Now I make more than enough money as an influencer to cover my modest monthly expenses, and I can still put some into savings. I'm no longer relying on my inheritance from Chris to live, and I see no reason I won't be able to continue living and traveling in my tiny house for the foreseeable future.

I'm not as happy as I used to be, living in Green Valley and looking forward to a long life with Chris, but I'm content. At peace. I'm usually glad to wake up to each new day. And for a while that was something I never believed could be true for me again.

After I drink my coffee, I do a half hour of yoga and then get out my camera to capture some images of the lake in the morning light and the surrounding woods clinging to the last of the year's green life.

Tee is expecting me by ten thirty, but I have time to put together one post, introducing my new location and highlighting the large lake, before I shower quickly and dress in a brown sweater, long plaid skirt, tights and boots. My dark brown hair is longer than it's ever been—almost reaching my waist—and it's currently threaded through with streaks of a rose-red color in various layers. The color changes fairly frequently whenever I get bored.

I French-braid the top layer of my hair around my crown, pleased with the effect and the way it brings attention to my dark eyes and high cheekbones, and leave the rest of my hair loose.

I'm never going to look like a fashion model. I never wear makeup, and my clothes are never in style. But I want to look as pretty as I can for some reason. I've been away for two years. I feel like a different person now. And I want the people who happen to see me to know I'm doing well.

When I'm satisfied with my appearance, I grab my big leather bag and head out the door, excited to see Tee and take her on errands and to lunch.

And hoping not to run into anyone too obnoxious while we're out.

~

Tee's house is an old farmhouse that was already getting old by the time Green Valley started being developed as an exclusive gated community on the lake fifty years ago. The house is a large two-story with a wraparound porch, and it looks like a ramshackle anachronism among the newer, nicer houses that surround it.

It still has a large yard and an outbuilding that used to be a barn but that Tee has always used as studio space for our arts and crafts.

I love this house. My earliest memories are set here, even before my parents died and I moved in with Tee full time when I was ten. A warm swell of pleasure fills me as I pull into the driveway and park in my regular spot on the far right of the gravel parking area.

After unbuckling and grabbing my bag, I slide down the high step from my pickup truck seat. As anyone who's ever met me would testify, I'm not a truck person, but I needed a heavy-duty vehicle to tow my tiny house around the country, so I ended up purchasing this one. I used to feel ridiculous—like some sort of impostor—driving it around, but I'm used to it now and don't care that it's not what anyone would expect of me.

Tee is opening the front door before I take my first step onto the paved walk. She's basically an older version of me—five-nine, still slender, tan skin, long salt-and-pepper hair. She's wearing a loose dress and a long hand-knit sweater. She grins and lifts her arms in welcome as I approach.

"Get over here, *mija*, and give your old Tee a hug!"

I pick up my speed, smiling as I run over to embrace her, overwhelmed with the familiar scent of her—cinnamon, paint, the lemon-based cleaner she's always used. I'm oddly emotional as I pull away. I have to give my eyes a quick swipe.

She notices. Of course she does. But she doesn't comment as she steps aside to let me in the house. "How does it feel to be back in Green Valley?"

"A little strange. But really okay. Not as hard as I expected."

"That's good." Tee and her sister, my maternal grandmother, were born in Mexico but moved to the US when they were in their late teens. She still has a very slight accent that's only noticeable occasionally. She eyes me up and down with a penetrating gaze I well remember. "I've missed you, but it looks like being away was the right thing for you. You're beautiful. And more settled in yourself. The last year has been good for you."

"I think so too. I feel more like myself. I'll probably always miss Chris, but I can actually see the shape of a life without him now."

Tee nods. "Daniela is in the studio. Give her a hug before we leave. I have a whole list of errands for today."

I'm not concerned about her list of errands. They usually consist of going by the post office to ship packages of her art or jewelry that she's sold online and visiting the art supply store and a few of her favorite boutiques downtown.

The post office I can tolerate, and the other stops will be as fun for me as they are for Tee.

My cousin, Daniela, is one year older than me. She's the only daughter of my mother's brother and his wife, who both died in the same accident that killed my parents. Daniela is built smaller than me and has more delicate features but the same mop of long dark hair. She's wearing a gray tank top and old army trousers but still manages to be gorgeous. She's tougher and more reserved than I've ever been, but we've always been close, and she's genuinely happy to see me when she glances up from the large chunk of wood she's chiseling.

After we hug and say a few words of greeting, she

explains she's deep into her work but that she hopes I'll hang out with her this afternoon.

I promise to do so and then walk with Tee back to the house so she can use the bathroom and apply lipstick before we leave.

It's an odd feeling. To be so completely at home. With family. And yet to feel like I'm not quite the same person I used to be when I was last here.

~

My errands with Tee proceed as I expect. The post office takes forever since it's almost Christmas, but we chat as we're waiting in line, so it doesn't feel like wasted time. After the onerous duty is done, we spend a long time in the art supply store, and I insist that Tee fill up a basket with anything she wants so I can buy it for her.

We have lunch at a little bistro downtown and then take our time browsing through some clothing stores. We mostly buy scarves and jewelry, but I do splurge on a wine-colored velvet jacket.

Whenever Tee expresses concern about my spending too much money, I try to explain how much money I'm earning as an influencer. It might as well be a foreign language to her, and she doesn't quiet down until I pull up my banking app and show her the balances in my checking and savings accounts.

She's quiet for a while after that. Then finally asks with a thoughtful frown, "Daniela shows me the pretty pictures you take and reads me your thoughts from her phone. They all sound just like you, so I always want to hear them. But I don't understand how you get paid for it. So people give you money just for being you?"

I think for a moment before I answer. "Yes. I guess that's a lot of it."

She shakes her head with a smile. "Well, it's very odd to me, but I'm proud of you. I should have expected you to make a unique place in the world for yourself, and now you have."

I hug her again, ridiculously pleased by her approval and understanding. I'm still smiling as I turn away and my eyes land on a familiar face.

It's a handsome face. Not like a movie star or a model but with a boy-next-door appeal. The jaw is square, the cheekbones strong, the forehead broad, and the mouth set in a frown. He's clean-shaven with slightly too long auburn hair that insists on curling despite his best attempts to tame it. His eyes are a vivid blue. His body is built naturally big and strong, although he's never spent a lot of time lifting weights. He's wearing gray trousers and a neat blue Oxford. He's standing on the corner of the sidewalk outside and was talking to someone else when our eyes met through the large front window of the shop.

Theo Humphrey.

Chris's best friend and the last person I want to see today.

I glance away, hoping futilely that he'll pretend he didn't see me and not come inside to speak. He's never liked me, and he's not going to have miraculously changed his opinion in the past two years. But he's never ignored me. He's always made a point to say a few terse, stilted words to me whenever our paths have crossed, as if he feels like it's his duty as Chris's friend to play nice.

So I'm not surprised when the bell on the door chimes a minute later. I turn around with as close to a polite smile as I can muster.

Theo blinks at me with a frown. "Maya."

"Theo Humphrey." I'm not sure why I always say his last name. Just that the name Humphrey sounds appropriate to his grumpy personality.

"You're back in town."

"It appears that way." I really can't help the dryness in my tone.

"How long?" There's still not a trace of a smile on his face. Just that sober, intent scrutiny he always focuses on me.

I shrug. "A few weeks. For the holidays."

"Maya," Tee says, stepping away from the rack she was searching through. "I don't see anything here." She pauses when she sees Theo. "Ah. You've found a young man."

My back stiffens sharply. "I do not have a young man.

Theo saw me as he was passing by and stopped in to be polite. You remember Chris's friend, Theo, don't you?"

Of course Tee remembers Theo. She remembers faces and names from decades back. I'm actually not sure whether she's trying to make me uncomfortable or Theo, but she's definitely doing it on purpose.

"How are you, Ms. Santiago?" Theo asks her soberly.

"Young man, you need to call me Tee like everyone else."

Theo clears his throat and doesn't answer her with anything but a nod.

I'm about to suggest Tee and I depart when Theo blurts out, "Are you still in that toy house?"

I narrow my eyes, offended despite my attempts not to care about his attitude. "It's not a toy house. It's a *tiny* house. And yes, I'm still living in it."

"Okay."

I wait a minute for him to say something else. To make a gesture toward basic civility.

But not Theo. He just stands there staring at me disapprovingly.

He's never been a big talker. Chris told me that, and I've seen it when he's interacted with other people. But he does manage to smile occasionally or have a normal conversation with people other than me. It's clearly only me he doesn't care for.

It used to really bother me, and maybe it still does. But

I'm no longer in a mental place where I'd try to remedy his opinion of me.

If he doesn't like me, then that's his problem. I've never done anything mean or impolite to him. Or even *around* him. I've always tried to be a good-hearted and generous person. I might not be the smartest or the most capable or the most ambitious or the most competent at life, but there are other positive qualities that people can possess.

If he can't appreciate who I am, then he's the only one it affects. I won't let it bother me anymore.

"Okay," I say, more glibly than I normally speak. "It was lovely to see you again, but Tee and I have to get going. Have a good day and a merry Christmas."

He kind of grunts. Maybe that's an answer. But it's clearly all I'm getting from him.

I take Tee's arm and maneuver her out of the shop before she decides to cause any trouble.

"A very shy young man, I believe," Tee says when we're out on the sidewalk.

I gasp and shoot her a surprised look. "Shy? No, not really. Rude is how I would describe him."

Tee gives a funny little laugh. "Is that what you think?"

"Of course that's what I think. He's always been that way with me—even back in school before I started dating Chris. It's not just that he didn't think I was a good match for his friend. He simply doesn't like me."

A memory hits me then of the first time I remember

Theo existing. I was in the sixth grade, and he was two grades above me in the same class as Chris. I didn't know either of them back then. I had a few friends but was never popular since I was new in town, my family wasn't wealthy in very wealthy Green Valley, and most people thought we were kind of odd.

But one afternoon some boys in my class were being mean to me, making fun of my clothes and that I spent every spare minute scribbling pictures in a notebook. One of them took my notebook from me and flipped through it, laughing meanly about my drawings.

Theo was striding by just then, and he elbowed the boy without even glancing over at him. The notebook dropped, and one glare from Theo, who was big and broad-shouldered even then, sent the other boys running.

He picked up my notebook and handed it to me. I smiled at him, shaky and touched and confused by the incident.

I did manage to say thank you, but he only shrugged and stared at me. I waited because it seemed like he was going to say something, but he never did.

He eventually shrugged again and walked off.

Over the years, I thought about that encounter, trying to fit it into my larger understanding of him. I tried smiling at him a few times after that. I wasn't flirting—definitely not—just trying to be nice since he'd helped me. But he never smiled back and never tried to talk to me.

When I started dating Chris in my sophomore year of high school, he finally began speaking to me but never in a friendly or genuine way. More like an unpleasant duty because of my connection to his best friend.

All I've been able to come up with in terms of an explanation is that Theo isn't a bad guy. He's a decent man who wants to help people who need it. He went to law school, and instead of taking a high-paying job, he became a public defender so he could help the people who need it the most.

That's probably how he viewed his rescue of me all those years ago. I needed help, so he helped me.

But that didn't mean he liked me then, and he definitely doesn't like me now.

I don't know why, but it's a fact of life that is clearly never going to change.

It doesn't matter. Other people like me. My life isn't defined by the one person who doesn't.

So Theo Humphrey can fade into my past. I'm not going to let him distract me from my otherwise enjoyable day.

He simply doesn't matter anymore.

2

That evening, I make myself wait to check for messages.

One of the things I've discovered in the past two years is that a primary source of stress in my life is the constant need to check my phone, to scroll social media for news or hits of stimulation, to be constantly *on*.

After Chris died, I mostly disconnected, but when my platform started to grow, I found myself getting obsessed again.

I had to force myself to limit my screen time to an hour in the morning and an hour in the evening. During the day, I'm brainstorming posts, taking photos, and drafting out reflections and meditations, but only twice a day do I post, scroll, and check messages. I will check text messages and calls throughout the day, but only my close circle can reach me that way.

Everyone else—including my pen pal—uses my social media accounts to connect with me.

More than once, I've been tempted to give him my private contact information, but I've talked myself out of it each time. That would make the correspondence real in a way it isn't right now. It would mean something, and I'm not ready for it to mean anything.

But every day I'm more and more excited to check my messages and see what he's said to me.

I make myself a quick panini for dinner and eat it outside, chatting with the retired couple whose RV is parked next to my house. I finish the chapter of the fantasy novel I've been reading. Then I finally let myself go inside and get on my computer.

I make this evening's post first. Then reply to several business-related inquiries. Then finally click on the bolded name: GVPioneer13.

The Pioneers are the Green Valley High School sports team's name. None of my followers know that I'm from Green Valley, so I have to assume this person is actually from the same town and knows who I am, at least in passing.

We probably weren't friends. If we were, why not come out and tell me his name? More likely, it's someone outside my circle who reached out randomly after noticing my success online and then fell into daily correspondence.

It's a man. I'm convinced of it. But I have no idea who or how old or whether our paths ever crossed in person.

The message is short this evening. He says he heard I was back in town and hopes I'm getting to connect with friends. He gives an update on the biography he's been reading. He asks me about this morning's post on how weird and unsettling it is to discover you're starting to heal from grief. And he explains he's got plans this evening and so doesn't have time for a longer message but he'll get up early tomorrow so he can write more.

I read the message over twice, quickly getting past my initial disappointment in the brevity of the note. I write back, asking how he heard I was back in town and then writing a paragraph responding to his comment on grief.

I've hit Send and am clearing out more messages when another reply from GVPioneer13 comes through.

A couple people mentioned you're back. More in the morning.

I frown, disappointed because this reply gives me no clues as to his identity. Why won't he just tell me who he is? After all, it's not like I've ever tried to make our online relationship romantic or sexual. He doesn't need to be afraid that, as soon as I get his name, I'll be pounding at his door and trying to throw myself at him.

I don't care if he's a multimillionaire—Green Valley has more than a few of them—or a groundskeeper or if he's just out of college or in his sixties. If he's married, it will be a little cringey since some of our messages have been emotionally intimate, but otherwise I can think of no reason not to tell me.

I've asked him directly, and all he's said is that it doesn't matter.

Honestly, it's getting a little frustrating.

With a surge of determination, I pull out the notebook I always carry around with me to jot down ideas or lists or sketches. I turn to an empty page and start making a new list.

Green Valley local

Pioneer (went to high school there???)

13 – Graduated in 2013? 13 on team? Moved to town at 13????

Reads biographies and historical nonfiction

Went to college. Maybe grad school. No idea where???

Only child

White

Knows about my art show senior year. Attended???

Met Chris

Still lives in Green Valley

Not an artist or a poet

Deep, intelligent, emotional, genuine, sensitive

With a sigh, I put down my pen and stare down at the items on the list. The last ones are characteristics I gleaned from our messages, but they don't really help me with his identity because they're characteristics that often aren't immediately obvious in a person.

The other items do narrow down possibilities considerably but not enough. Because Green Valley kids so often stick around after school or move back after college and grad school, there are far too many people I know who fit this list.

He could be dozens of men.

My best guess is he was probably in school with Chris and me. Maybe in one of our years or else only a couple of years before or after us. He seems so familiar with my history, and his experiences in Green Valley very closely match my own.

So maybe I'll start with that. Tomorrow I can get my hands on some yearbooks and begin writing out names.

Pleased with this resolution, I finish my work online, too distracted to do any scrolling or research tonight. Then I close down my laptop and start my winding-down routine. Yoga. Shower and pajamas. Herbal tea with relaxing music and a snuggle with Claude and Ed. Then I brush, floss, do my skin regimen, and get into bed to read a few more chapters before I go to sleep.

My mind doesn't want to turn off this evening. At first I think it's because of the frustration of not being able to identify my pen pal, but the face I keep seeing, the conversations I keep rehearsing, when I close my eyes all belong to Theo Humphrey.

The following day, my eyes pop open before seven o'clock. Normally, if I wake up too early, I'll try to doze for another hour, but this morning my mind leaps into action, so there's no reason not to get up.

I try to go through my relaxed morning routine of lemon water, walk, meditation, and yoga, but resting my mind simply isn't happening today. I finally give up, make coffee in my French press, and sit down with my laptop to see what's going on in the world.

My pen pal has already written back as he promised, telling me a funny story about a coworker who chides anyone who makes unexpected noises like sneezes or laughs and reported him for letting out an exclamation when he stubbed his toe.

I giggle over his description. He sounds more amused than angry about it, although I can imagine getting reported over such a thing would be incredibly annoying.

He goes on to talk about a Christmas when he was a boy. He was getting suspicious of Santa's existence and so was determined to get proof one way or another. After his parents went to bed, he snuck outside and set up a strategic position on the back steps, bundled up in a blanket and staring at the sky until he finally fell asleep. His mom found him out there in the morning, still sleeping.

I'm touched by the little story, and I immediately send a message back, responding to both the coworker and the past Christmas story and then confessing I never believed in Santa but used to pretend I did so I could fit in with the other kids. I also mention that I'm not much in the Christmas spirit this year, but I'm going to try to conjure a more festive mood, so I'm planning to watch the carolers who have been singing in the town park every day at lunchtime this week.

Part of me hopes he'll take the hint and show up to confess. If not, it's still a normal thing I might mention in our daily messages.

I read over my note once before I send it to catch any obvious errors. Then I start working on my posts for the day. One is a very nice photo of the gray winter lake with a reflection on how all the artificial cheer of our commercial Christmases has stolen for us the instinctive solemnity of the season that nature itself guides us toward. The other is a reel of the creative ways I fit all my winter sweaters into my tiny home.

When I finish, it's not even nine o'clock and I've done everything I need to do this morning. My brain still won't let me rest, so I shower and dress to go hang out with Tee for the morning.

. . .

Later, at a few minutes before noon, I'm on the sidewalk downtown on my way to the park. I've got three packages to mail for Tee, a thermos of spiced tea she insisted I bring, my sketch pad, and a bag with the sandwich I just bought.

I'm juggling everything relatively well, but I'm not stable enough to withstand the bump and startled jerk when a door opens onto the sidewalk from a popular local coffee shop.

The packages and my sketch pad scatter on the ground. With a combination of luck and effort, I manage to hold on to my thermos and my lunch.

I let out a breathless exclamation, more surprised than upset by the altercation. But then I see a stunned, frowning Theo glaring at me, still holding the door to the coffee shop open.

"Oh. Oh, I'm sorry," I say reflexively even though it's quite clear I did nothing wrong.

"It's fine," he mutters, still standing frozen, his shoulder propping open the door and his eyes fixed disapprovingly on me.

It's fine, he says. As if he's being incredibly gracious in making allowances for my clumsiness.

Trying not to make a face at him, I lean over to collect my stuff.

Unfortunately, he leans down at the same time, and we bump heads. Not gently.

"Ow!" I straighten up abruptly, rubbing my head and

trying to clear the pain from my brain. "I'm sorry. What a mess."

"It's fine," he says again, frowning even more deeply as he bends back over to pick up my packages.

It's fine. As if, yet again, it's all my fault.

I lean over to retrieve my sketch pad. Some of the pages are crumpled, so I try to smooth them out.

He watches me with that same grumpy detachment, as if I'm an alien creature for caring about the state of sketches I've worked very hard on.

"I'll carry these," he mumbles, nodding down at the packages he's still holding.

"I can—"

"I've got 'em."

I want to argue because I want to get rid of this man as quickly as possible, but he's as stubborn as a mule. He always has been. And having a debate about who is going to carry my packages will only serve to extend our time together.

He falls into step with me as I continue. Maybe he can guess where I'm heading or maybe he doesn't care, because he doesn't question me at all as we walk into the park and find a bench.

I put down my bag and thermos before reaching for the packages. "Thank you," I tell him, trying to sound cool instead of completely frazzled. "Although I could have gotten them fine."

Theo just stands and stares at me, rubbing the side of his forehead where we collided earlier.

What the hell is his problem? It's not my fault he opened the door right into me. Is he really all mad about it?

For the first time, I notice he's got a paper bag tucked in his pocket. It looks like the right size for a sandwich from the coffee shop. He must have stopped there to grab some lunch.

As I'm setting down the packages, one slips off the bench onto the ground again. I sure hope there's nothing fragile in them.

Before I can lean over, Theo reaches for it and sets it in a more stable position.

Even that annoys me. Like he's trying to prove I'm clumsy and incompetent in the most basic of actions.

"Okay," I say at last. "I'm going to sit here and listen to the carolers." I wait for a moment as Theo does more staring. "I'm pretty sure I can handle it on my own."

He gives me a short nod, turns on his heel, and walks away.

Not for the first time, I wonder how Chris put up with the man. He can't even make a pretense of civility with me.

I watch his straight back, broad shoulders, and long legs as he strides away, trying to dismiss him from my mind.

But for some reason, he won't be dismissed.

That evening, I've planned to meet Daniela at a coffee shop at six fifteen. She's been working as an administrative assistant at a local art gallery for the past few years, and her shift ends at six. Like the rest of the family, she's not inclined toward regular office work, so it's hardly her dream job, but she likes that the gallery at least connects her to art and artists.

She's always been more talented and ambitious in art than I ever was.

The coffee shop where we're meeting has been around since high school, and it's clearly still a popular place. Most of the tables are full when I arrive, and there are a few people in line in front of me.

Waiting never bothers me. I'm not an impatient person. I amuse myself as I stand in line by looking around, waving at an older lady who is a longtime friend of Tee, and nodding at the owner of the art supply store.

There's a large table in the far corner with a bunch of people I recognize from school. Not friends but acquaintances. They don't see me, and I don't make an effort to catch their attention.

When I reach the counter, I turn around and blink when I recognize Chase Park taking orders. He was in my year of school, and I always liked him. A laid-back, good-natured guy with the bland, unfocused manner of a stoner or a surfer. I learned early on that he's far more intelligent than he conveys. I wouldn't have made it through the coding class I took on a whim if he hadn't sat beside me and been willing to help.

My surprise isn't that he's still in town but that he's still working at this coffee shop. He bused tables here back in high school.

"You're still here," I say without thinking.

His shoulders shake in a silent laugh that's reflected in his eyes but not his mouth. "I have gone home a few times in the past ten years."

"Sorry." I shake my head with a smile. "I didn't mean it to sound like that."

"No worries. I'm not offended."

I can tell he means it. He's one of the most unruffled people I've ever known.

"It is kind of funny to think I might be a cursed soul trapped behind this counter serving Green-Valleyites coffee for eternity like poor Prometheus," he goes on.

"You probably have it a little better than Prometheus," I say with another smile, recognizing he's joking despite his sober expression. Someone as smart as Chase could have gotten another job if he'd wanted one, so he must still be here by choice.

"I'm way better off than Prometheus."

Peering at his attractive face and mobile mouth, I recognize some sort of energy simmering under the surface of his bland expression. Something new. Something that wasn't there when I saw him last. "You look happy," I say, blurting the words out without thinking it through, which is one of my unfortunate habits.

He gives another one of those silent chuckles. "I am happy."

"I'm glad."

"It looks like the past two years have been good for you too."

"I think they have been. I needed to get away."

"And are you planning to stay away?"

I shrug. "Probably. Although I'm going to try to visit more often now that I'm on better emotional footing." When a man comes in and stands in line behind me, looking impatient, I order my herbal tea and cranberry-orange scone.

Chase winks at me after I pay.

Since he appears to be manning the shop all alone this evening and it will probably be a few minutes before my order is ready, I don't wait at the counter. Instead, I turn toward the room to find a table for Daniela and me.

The big table has seen me now. A former classmate named Paige is waving at me, summoning me over to the empty seat at their table.

I walk over but don't sit down, greeting everyone and explaining I'm meeting my cousin.

In addition to Paige, I recognize Dan Mills, Rafe and

Jules Archibald, and Carlton Hill. I say hello to Dan's newish wife, Vicky. After a few minutes of small talk, Paige starts to ask me about my art, photography, and jewelry.

I answer easily, but it feels like there's a purpose behind her questioning. I don't realize what it is until Chase comes over with my tea and scone, setting it on the table in front of where I'm standing and then walking over behind Paige. He squeezes her shoulder and then slides his hand to gently span the side of her neck. "Maybe let her get her bearings before you start recruiting her for your site," he murmurs.

My recollection of Paige is as a hardworking, ambitious student who strove to excel at everything. She's always been nice to me, but we've never had anything in common. It makes much more sense that she's working on building her business rather than making idle conversation about my art.

I appreciate that she thinks my work is of value enough to recruit, and I'm about to ask for her contact information when I suddenly realize something. "Wait!" I blink at Paige. At Chase, whose hand is still tucked under her hair. "You two are together?"

The others at the table laugh at my blunt inquiry. Paige smiles. "We are. Since last Christmas."

"I never would have put you two together, but you know, it fits perfectly." I glance up at Chase, who is still simmering with that undercurrent of excitement. "No wonder you're so happy."

Chase isn't embarrassed by the comment. I don't remember him ever being embarrassed by anything. He's about to say something, but then his eyes move to the front door. "There's your cousin. And I better get back to work."

I wave at Daniela and then turn back to Paige.

Ever efficient, she's already pulled out a card and hands it to me.

It's an old-fashioned business card with her name and contact information as well as the information for her business, a centralized website for local arts and crafts. "Maybe we can touch base sometime soon," she says with a smile.

I tell her I'll be in touch and then grab a table for two for Daniela and me.

Daniela is always tired getting off from work because the administrative duties wear on her personality. But she makes an effort to be in a good mood for me, and we have a good time catching up and hearing about each other's lives.

After about an hour, I can tell she's exhausted. "Have you looked around for a job that isn't so much administrative work?" I ask her.

She shrugs and leans back in her chair. I've always thought she was prettier than me, and her dark eyelashes are unnaturally thick and long. "I keep looking but so far nothing that would be easier on me than this one is. At least with this job I can sometimes talk to artists and make connections with buyers and collectors."

"Yeah, that's something anyway."

"I really just need to marry a rich man so I can make art to my heart's content and not have to worry about a paycheck."

I laugh at that, as I'm supposed to. But I can tell she's only half joking. Daniela has never been romantic. She's never dreamed of falling in love or having a fairy-tale romance. If she stumbled on a semidecent man with money who made her an offer, she'd probably accept it.

"Did you notice that Theo came in about thirty minutes ago?" she asks out of the blue.

I stiffen and turn my head to look behind me, realizing she's right. There is Theo, sitting at the big table with Paige and the others.

I didn't know he was friends with them. Obviously, I know in theory that he has friends—after all, Chris was his best one most of their lives—but he's so unfriendly that I can't imagine many people would want to hang out with him for any length of time.

He appears engaged in conversation, so maybe he exerts himself with people other than me.

When his gaze drifts over toward me, I quickly look away.

"Does he hang out with them a lot?" I ask Daniela. He got his lunch from here earlier. Maybe he just likes this place and they happen to be here too.

She lifts her shoulders. "Not all the time. I've seen him with them a few times lately. Losing Chris was hard on him, but he seems to be socializing more lately."

I try not to make a face.

"I'm not saying it was as hard for him as it was for you, but it's hard when your best friend dies."

"I know it is. And I'd never question that his friendship with Chris was real. I just wish he hadn't always acted like I was..."

When I trail off, Daniela arches her eyebrows. "Like you were what?"

"Like I wasn't good enough for Chris."

"Yeah, I don't know why he always acted that way. He's not the friendliest soul in the universe, but he's usually not so frowny as he is around you." She sighs. "Some people just don't click."

"I guess." I shake my head. "Anyway, it doesn't matter. By the way, do you have your old yearbooks?"

"What? No, of course not. Why would I have kept those?"

It probably was a silly question. Daniela is an unsentimental as it's possible to be.

"Just checking. I went by the high school, and they let

me look at the ones for the years I was in school, but I really want to borrow some so I can take them with me and study them."

"Why don't you ask at that table?" She nods back toward the others. "I bet one of them kept them."

I sigh. That's exactly what I was planning to do, but Theo's presence has discouraged me.

It's irrational not to follow my original plan simply because of Theo Humphrey, however. So after Daniela and I carry our dishes to the counter and I say goodbye to her, I wander back over to the big table.

When they all stare up at me, I ask, "Does anyone still have their yearbooks from high school?"

They look at me blankly, evidently taken by surprise by the abrupt question.

"I do," Theo says. "Did you want to borrow them?"

Of course it would be him. I try to keep a pleasant expression as I turn my eyes to him. "I would if you don't mind."

"I don't mind." He stands up, reaching down to grab his old leather laptop bag from the floor.

"Oh, you don't have to get them now! I can grab them some other—"

"I was done here. I can grab 'em for you now." His coffee cup is indeed empty, and he's already standing up. "See y'all later."

The others appear amused—either by my sudden request or Theo's abrupt departure. I smile and wave at them as I steel my spirit to have a polite conversation with this man.

"I'm just a couple blocks away from here," he says as we leave the coffee shop. "I can go get them if you want to wait here."

"I can walk with you," I say with a perfectly civil smile. "That way you won't have to come all the way back."

He nods and starts down the sidewalk. He's not smiling or looking at me or attempting to make conversation as we walk. I fall into step with him, having to take longer strides than normal to keep up.

After a few minutes, I'm annoyed. He could slow down or say something or crack a smile or something.

Yes, he's doing me a favor, but still.

"What do you need the yearbooks for?" he asks without segue when we turn onto a street off the downtown blocks that has newish town houses and apartments.

"I'm just looking for someone."

"Who?"

I don't answer. Not only because he's so presumptuous in demanding I tell him but also because I'm kind of self-conscious about admitting I have a secret pen pal.

What if he misinterprets my interest and thinks I'm betraying Chris?

He turns his head to peer at me sharply.

I keep my expression blank.

"You were on the chess team in high school, weren't you?"

He frowns. "Yes."

"Do you remember someone in it who liked *Count of Monte Cristo*?"

His eyebrows shoot up. "What?"

"You heard me, I think."

"Why would—"

"It's just a question."

He's still frowning, but thoughtfully now. Like he's searching his memory. "No one comes to mind."

"Okay."

"You're looking for someone on the chess team?"

"He might not be on the chess team. It was just an idea."

"What the hell is all this about? You searching for a long-lost love or something?"

I've managed to trap myself in this conversation. I can either tell him or let him imagine something wrong and ridiculous.

"No, of course not. But someone has been writing to me and won't tell me who they are, so I'm trying to figure it out."

"Ah." His expression relaxes slightly. Evidently he

doesn't believe this situation is as absurd as he might have. "So that's why you need the yearbooks?"

"Yes."

He's silent for a minute until he turns toward a small apartment building that looks to house no more than eight units. "This is me. You want to come up?"

I really don't want to visit his apartment. "I can just wait down here if you don't mind bringing them down to me."

"Okay." He walks in the front door, and I wait outside until he returns a few minutes later, carrying four bound books.

I accept them when he hands them to me. "Thank you."

He stares down at me, still unsmiling. "I can help if you want."

"Help with what?"

"Find this person you're looking for."

"Why would you help?"

He gives a slight half shrug. "Doing a favor for Chris's girl."

Chris's girl.

That's who I used to be, but that's not me anymore.

But there's no reason Theo would know or care about that fact.

"I'll let you know if I need help," I tell him. "Thanks for the offer."

He nods. Stares at me some more. Then turns abruptly back toward the front door. "Bye."

I huff with dry amusement. He's just as friendly as ever. "Okay. See you later."

He waves back at me briefly before he disappears through the door.

3

THE NEXT DAY IS SATURDAY, AND I TAKE TEE OUT TO breakfast at eight.

Eight is her idea of a late, leisurely weekend breakfast. If she had her choice, she'd be showing up at our favorite pancake place at six in the morning.

Because I was able to talk her into a later breakfast, I'm able to go through my regular morning routine—only slightly abbreviated—before I take the walk into downtown and reach the restaurant only a few minutes late.

Naturally, Tee is already there and at a table with a pot of coffee ready for us.

I hug and kiss her before I sit down.

"Did you walk all the way, Maya? It's much too far, and it's cold out."

"It's less than two miles, and it's not that cold today. Plus I'm all bundled up." That much is the truth. It takes a couple of minutes for me to unwind my scarf, pull off my gloves and cap, and unbutton the long wool coat I'm wearing over my stretchy jeans and long sweater.

Tee is smiling as I settle myself and get comfortable.

"What is it?" I ask after a minute.

"Nothing, mija. Just that you always come in with a minor flurry wherever you go. You spill over into every space. I've missed it."

It's impossible to see her fond expression and believe she's criticizing me, although in the past I've been a bit embarrassed by this particular trait of mine. Some people are able to move through the world without making a single ripple. Efficient and streamlined with a minimal footprint on their surroundings.

That's not me.

Chris used to tease me about how it was his job to try to contain me. Otherwise I might lose parts of myself everywhere I go.

I raise my hips slightly so I can smooth down the tail of my sweater, and then I can finally stop adjusting. "What are you thinking about for breakfast?"

We have a brief conversation about whether the key lime French toast or the gingerbread pancakes are a better option. By the time the server comes over, we've decided to get one of each order and share.

That resolved, I reach down to my big bag and pull out one of the yearbooks I borrowed from Theo. I spent a couple of hours last night scouring through the pages, making notes and whittling down a list of about forty possible names.

Forty.

"Feeling nostalgic?" Tee asks, nodding at where I set the yearbook on the table.

"No. I was actually hoping for your help to see what you know about some people."

This comment naturally leads to a number of questions, so I have to explain the situation as well as I can, my attempt to remain vague foiled by Tee's intrigued curiosity. Our food arrives by the time she's finally satisfied as to why I'm asking her about random former schoolmates.

The list includes everyone I couldn't immediately cross off for obvious reasons and who basically fit the criteria I've laid out for my pen pal as well as those I know nothing about in order to judge. Tee suggests going over the list quickly at first so she can help eliminate more of them.

She's able to help me get rid of eleven names right away—most of whom have moved away since high school. As we eat, we cross off a few more and organize the remaining twenty-four into two different lists. More likely and less likely.

I'm pleased as I gaze down at my new shorter list of twelve most likely possibilities when our plates and the coffeepot are empty. This is a much more workable number. I might actually be able to come up with a solution to this mystery if this is the list of options.

"It's a rather odd thing for you to be focused on right now, isn't it?" Tee asks, her sharp eyes scrutinizing my face.

"Is it odd? It's a puzzle, and I want to figure it out."

"I understand that, but this is a lot of time and mental effort to be putting into a purely intellectual pursuit."

I laugh at her wording. "It's more than intellectual, of course. It's bugging me. I like this person, and I don't understand why he won't tell me who he is. I don't like not knowing."

"I can understand that. I'm curious too. But are you sure it's not more than that?"

"What do you mean?"

"Are you maybe having feelings for this person?"

I know what she's asking. And it makes perfect sense to be asking me.

But I don't know how to answer her.

"I didn't mean to upset you," she murmurs when I don't reply for a minute.

"I'm not upset. Not really. But it's not a simple question. I do have some feelings for this person, but they could mean anything. I don't know enough about him to have any sort of well-defined feelings."

"Of course you don't. You're still young, and you've healed after losing Chris. It's natural to have feelings, and they currently don't have a target, so maybe it's become this person."

"I think that's probably right. I've been content. I really have. I think I'd be okay being single for the rest of my life. But that's not what I really want. So maybe it's loneliness and isolation that's turned this random mystery person into... into someone I want."

"That could be it. Or maybe there is real potential there. But I simply can't see it going anywhere if the person insists on hiding."

"You're right. Of course you're right. But I feel like I still need to know. Just so I can move on."

Tee nods, thinking silently for a stretch of time until she finally concludes, "That makes sense to me. So I'll help you as much as I can. Let me see the pictures of these people. Maybe the photos will spark more memories."

We spend another fifteen minutes reviewing the pictures of the twelve remaining names on my list. I'm having a good time chatting with her and recalling every random anecdote I can to provide context for some of these guys when her eyes move over my shoulder.

"There's someone who might be able to help us."

Confused and surprised, I turn in my chair to look.

Theo Humphrey.

Of course it is.

He must have been in here for a while, eating with an unkempt guy in his early twenties. They are both standing next to their table, and Theo is shaking the other guy's hand. They start to leave, but then Theo glances over to us and catches Tee's eye.

He says something to his companion and walks over here as the other guy leaves the restaurant.

"Good morning," he says, unsmiling as he reaches us. He's focused on Tee, who gestured him over here. He gives me a couple of quick glances but nothing else.

"We need your help, Theodore."

"We don't really," I murmur, embarrassed and shooting her a significant look.

She blithely ignores both the look and my words. "She's trying to track someone down."

"Yes, I know. She borrowed my yearbooks to conduct her investigation."

"Oh, did she?" Tee arches her eyebrows at me. "Then have a seat for a few minutes and help us."

"Tee," I begin.

This time both she and Theo ignore my attempt to forestall his participation. He pulls out one of the extra chairs at our table and sits down. He's dressed in khakis, an untucked button-up shirt, and a canvas jacket.

He looks good. More relaxed and casual than yesterday. He didn't even shave this morning, and the stubble gives him a rugged look I'm not used to seeing on him.

He's reached for the list on the page of my notebook, and he studies it wordlessly for a minute.

"You can cross off these two," he says at last, pointing toward the third and the eighth name on the list.

"Why is that?"

"You said this person is a fan of *Count of Monte Cristo*, right? These two probably never finished a book in their lives."

Tee snickers at his dry tone, and even I can't deny the logic of his rationale. I neatly draw lines through the two names.

"See, I told you he'd be helpful. What else do you think?"

Theo shakes his head, his eyes focused down on the page. "I don't know the others very well."

I sigh. "Me either."

"I guess we'll have to talk to them."

My shoulders stiffen. "What do you mean?"

"If you want to conduct a thorough investigation, then we'll have to do some interviews. What do you think I mean?"

"I mean, you're planning to do them with me?"

"Why wouldn't I?"

My mouth drops open. I turn toward Tee, who is visibly trying to refrain from laughing. "Because it's not your thing. It's mine."

"But you'll do better to have a detached observer to help you sort through the evidence."

"I'm detached!"

He shakes his head at me, his mouth twitching just slightly.

For some reason, his expression makes me want to smile.

I don't, of course. That would reward him for his obnoxious behavior.

"I'm capable of solving this mystery on my own," I say.

"Of course you are, mija," Tee says comfortingly. "But if he's willing to help, why shouldn't he?"

I sigh. If Tee has something in her head, nothing is going to get her to give it up. And I simply don't have the energy or the will for a fight. "Fine. He can help a little."

"Good." Tee starts putting on her coat. "Why don't you walk her home, Theodore? She walked all this way on her own. That will give you a chance to discuss everything."

"Tee—"

"Now don't argue. He's not busy today, are you?"

"No. I was meeting with a client just now, but I don't have anything else today." He's almost—almost—smiling. He clearly likes Tee.

A lot more than he likes me.

"So there. He'll walk you home, Maya, and you can go over your list. You only have ten left. You can surely find an answer soon."

After we say goodbye to Tee, I stay long enough to pay for our breakfast, and then Theo and I walk out of the restaurant together.

It's a brisk, sunny morning, and I like the cool, fresh air as I breathe it in. It's not even nine thirty yet on a Saturday morning in December. Most of the downtown shops and restaurants aren't open yet, so the streets and sidewalks are mostly empty. The streetlight posts that line the roads are festooned with garlands and snowflakes that light up at night. There are a few new signs and storefronts from the Green Valley I remember, but the scene is still familiar. Pleasant.

Like home.

When I look back at Theo, I catch him watching me. "What is it?"

He shakes his head. "Why did you stay away for so long?"

I shrug, uncomfortable by the question. I'm generally a fairly open and honest person. I don't mind sharing myself with other people, whether or not we're particularly close. I don't have a lot of boundaries and hang-ups about keeping my thoughts to myself, which is why I've been able to so easily fall into sharing private reflections with such a huge number of followers.

But it's different writing a post online and sending it out to faceless numbers. That feels like less of a risk than answering Theo's question.

Because it's Theo. Someone I've known forever but never liked or trusted.

I'm not the kind of person who is able to put on a mask, so I either have to shut him down completely or else give him a genuine answer.

Shutting him down would be rude. It would feel mean, and that's not me. He's been helping me for whatever reason, so surely I owe him basic civility.

"I don't know," I say at last. "I guess I was kind of afraid."

"Afraid of what?" He's looking at me for real. Seeing me. His expression is sober and thoughtful.

At the moment, he doesn't seem scowly and aloof. It feels like he's really listening to me.

Which makes it safe enough for me to admit, "I was afraid if I came back I'd be... I'd be drowned in grief again. That being around all the places and people connected to Chris would be too much for me."

"And is it?" he asks quietly. "Are you drowning?"

I shake my head. "I still feel sad sometimes. I miss him. But it's different now. Green Valley still feels like home to me, but somehow it feels like it's moved on the way I have."

He doesn't answer immediately, but when I shoot him a quick look, it's clear he's thinking about what I said. "Yeah. I guess it feels that way to me too even though I never went away. Like the town has reshaped itself without him."

The choice of words hit me strangely. My throat tightens and my eyes burn. "In a way, it doesn't seem right. It's not fair that the void he left in the world gets filled eventually. He was important enough that that empty space should remain forever, but I guess that's not how life works."

"No." Theo shifts strangely, making a weird gesture with his hand. Like he started to reach out but changed his mind. "It's not right, but it happens anyway."

"Do you have another best friend now?" I've been looking downward—at my boots and his shoes against the sidewalk—but I glance up as I ask the question.

He works his jaw briefly. "No. I don't." He waits a beat before he asks, "Have you found someone else to love?"

I shake my head. "No."

For some reason, this brief, stilted exchange makes me feel closer to Theo than I ever have before. Chris was an only child, and his parents are shallow and self-involved. If anyone in the world misses Chris the way I do and understands the poignancy of the world going on without him, it's Theo.

He takes a slightly raspy breath. Then he puts a light hand on his mouth as we start to walk in the direction of my campground. As we start, he reaches over to unhook the strap of my big bag from my shoulder so he can carry it for me.

I'm surprised by the gesture, but it must be second

nature for him. Like rescuing me from the bullies back in school. He does it because that's the way he's been raised, whether the other person means something to him or not.

"Do you want to?" he asks after we've made it down two blocks in silence.

"Do I want to what?"

"Find someone else to love."

There's nothing hostile or accusatory in the question, but it rouses my defenses anyway. "Why wouldn't I?"

"I don't know. I was just asking if you'd thought about it."

"Of course I've thought about it." My voice sounds tired —exhausted—to my own ears. "I'm twenty-eight years old. I'd like to find someone to spend my life with. Start a family with. I wanted that with Chris, and the desire doesn't go away just because the person it was supposed to happen with is gone."

"It might go away. I don't much want to have another best friend again."

I breathe heavily as I look up at him, trying to figure out whether he thinks I'm wrong to move on from Chris. "Just because you might want to close yourself down now doesn't mean it's the proper response or that I'll necessarily feel the same way."

"I wasn't saying—"

"I get that it might be hard for you. To see me with someone else. That it might feel like a betrayal of Chris to you or something. But I... I can't make my life an empty monument to what he should have been."

"I'm not saying or implying that you should." He sounds gruff now. He's probably annoyed by my defensiveness. "So there is someone you're interested in?"

"No," I admit. "But there might be. One day. I know you've never liked me and you might not want to see it, but Chris wouldn't want me to spend the rest of my life alone."

"I know he wouldn't." He's gruffer than ever, the words coming out with a low rumble in his throat. He jerks his head to the side, looking away from me. "I know that."

I feel like I want to cry and like I want to jump out of my skin at the same time. I haven't felt this way—so pulled to the edge emotionally—in a really long time, and it's both scary and weirdly exciting.

The fear takes precedence. I rub my face and give myself a shake, like I might be able to physically shed the intense emotions. "Anyway, I don't know why we're even talking about this." I honestly can't remember if he brought it up or I did. "You really don't have to walk me back and help with my pen pal investigation just because Tee pushed you into it."

"I don't mind. You've got me kind of interested in it too now."

I shrug. Evidently it's too much to hope for that he'd step back into the shadows of my life just because it would make me more comfortable.

"Plus maybe you could do a favor for me in return."

I narrow my eyes. "I never asked you for help with this, but you're expecting me to do something for you in return."

"It seems like the polite thing to do." His mouth is twitching slightly again in that way I saw earlier. The way that makes me want to smile.

"It seems like the obnoxious thing to do," I mutter. Then, mostly out of curiosity, I add, "What did you want in return?"

"Chris's folks gave me a couple of boxes of his old stuff when they were clearing out their house to sell. I've kept them in one of my closets without even opening them, but it feels like I should do something with the stuff. You want to help me go through it sometime?"

I don't need to ask why his parents didn't give the stuff to me. They never liked or approved of me. They'd been hoping Chris would choose the daughter of one of Green Valley's wealthier families to marry so they could tie their family to a fortune.

And they were furious Chris changed his will and life insurance beneficiary to me as soon as we got engaged.

Of course they wouldn't give me any of Chris's belongings even if they were simply hoping to get rid of them.

"Yeah," I tell Theo. "I'll help you go through them."

"You want to do it soon or wait until after the holidays?"

I take a breath and come to my answer quickly. "Let's do it right away, if you don't mind. I'd like to get the hard stuff done before Christmas."

"You got it. Why don't you come over to my place this afternoon? We can get it done today."

∽

So later that day, at just after three thirty, I show up at Theo's apartment building.

He has to buzz me in the main door, and I walk upstairs to his unit on the second floor. His place is a nice-enough one bedroom in a fairly new complex. It's nothing fancy or luxurious, but it's got a small, updated kitchen and a decent-size balcony.

His furnishings are good quality but minimal—a leather couch, one upholstered chair, a side table, a large television on the wall, and a desk in the main room since there are no available rooms for a home office. Every available surface is covered with stacks of books.

When I've scanned the place, Theo lifts his eyebrows at me. "Well? What's your verdict?"

"It's got potential, but you really need some art on the walls and a couple of area rugs. Did you just move in? How long have you lived here?"

"A year and a half," he admits dryly.

I choke on a laugh. "What's your grudge against colors? Everything is brown."

"I like brown."

"Of course you do."

"If you want to pick out art for the walls, I'd be happy to buy and hang it, but you've got to already know I'd be useless at figuring it out for myself."

"I suspected." I'm blushing slightly at the idea of picking out art for Theo's apartment. It feels like an intimate thing to do, so why do I like the idea of it?

"You want something to drink?"

"I'll take some water." I nod toward the two big cardboard boxes set on the floor in front of the couch. "Is this them?"

"Yeah."

He goes to pour us both some water while I take a seat on the couch. It is a very comfortable couch. I have to give him that much.

When he comes to sit beside me, I sip the water while he leans over to open the closest box.

Inside is a motley assortment of Chris's stuff from his childhood bedroom. He had everything that really mattered to him in the apartment I cleared out after he died, but he'd obviously left some stuff at his parents' house. That's what's in these boxes.

We pull out textbooks, school notebooks, posters he had on his wall, worn T-shirts, a pair of old sneakers, trophies from track meets he placed in, a framed certificate for being the all-star on the debate team during senior year, some old beer bottles he saved from college. Even the bedding from his bed.

"They must have just piled everything from his room into here," I say at last, looking at the assorted stuff around us after we empty both boxes.

"Yeah. Maybe they kept something, but I can't see what." He smiles down at one of the posters for a local band that was popular when we were in high school. "Most of this stuff didn't mean anything to him."

"Yeah. He wouldn't have left it in their house if it did. I think we can probably trash most of it, unless you want to keep it for some reason. I mean, all these notebooks…" I flip through a couple of them, but there's nothing in them but some school notes and a few silly sketches. I find one he did of me and tear out the page so I can keep it.

"We can probably give away the bedding and some of the books to the thrift shop. But these shirts are too old for anyone to want."

"They weren't even ones he really liked. Let's just throw them out."

We get through with school stuff, the bedding and the clothing, sorting between trash and giveaway.

Then Theo picks up a trophy, shaking his head at it.

"He didn't care about those silly trophies."

"No." Decided, he chucks the rest of them into the box we identified as trash.

I'm inspecting one of the beer bottles when I glance over to see Theo looking down at the poster again. "Keep that if you want. Y'all went to a ton of their concerts."

Theo nods and rolls it up neatly. "You keeping the bottles?"

"I don't think so. Why on earth would he have kept them?"

"Two of them y'all drank on a date to a waterfall somewhere? The other ones were on your nineteenth birthday."

I stare down at the bottles, my throat tightening again. The date to the waterfall was when he first told me he loved me. My nineteenth birthday was the first time we had sex.

Chris wasn't a particularly sentimental man, but he loved me, and he kept these on purpose because of what I meant to him.

I blink down at the bottles until I've recovered. "I'll keep these," I manage to rasp.

"Okay." Theo is still for a minute until I'm able to look back up at him. Then he holds up the old sneakers.

I shrug. "Just toss them, I guess."

We make it through everything else fairly quickly, and nothing else evokes another storm of emotion. Theo closes both boxes by tucking in the flaps on alternating sides and then scrawls TRASH on one and GIVEAWAY on the other.

"There," he says. "That's done. Thanks for helping."

"You're welcome. Thanks for saving them."

We sit in silence side by side on the couch, both of us staring down at the boxes. After a stretch of time, Theo asks gruffly, "You okay?"

I glance over, but he's not even looking at me. "I'm okay. What about you?"

"I'm okay too."

"Okay. Good." I swallow. "Okay."

We're saying okay too much, but I don't know what else to say. I don't know why I feel close to Theo right now—closer than I ever would have imagined I could. I've never even liked the man. Why do I feel like I know him better than almost anyone else? Why do I feel like we're somehow together in this when we've never been together in anything?

"I guess that's it then," I say at last.

"Yeah. I guess so. Thanks again."

"Sure." I make myself stand up because who knows what I'll do or say if I linger here much longer. "You still want to help me talk to the guys on that list? You really don't have to."

"I know I don't have to, but I've got nothing better to do tomorrow. We might as well see if we can track down as many as we can." He stands up too since I'm obviously getting ready to leave.

I nod. "Okay then. Thanks. I'll text you tomorrow morning when I'm ready to get going. It won't be too early."

"I'll be ready anytime after eight."

"Right." I give myself a little shake as I reach for my bag. "I'll take off then."

He nods. "See you."

Since there's absolutely nothing else to say, I get out of there fast.

4

Theo and I have picked out four of the ten guys on my list who we can probably run into casually—just by chance—sometime during the day on a Sunday.

The first one is Mick Bradford, who attends early Mass at one of the Catholic churches every week. I only have vague memories of Mick from school, but Theo is absolutely certain of his faithful church attendance.

Since the early service at this church ends at nine thirty, Theo and I are sitting on a bench nearby at nine twenty-five, drinking the coffee he got us from the coffee shop and pretending to be simply passing by.

It's probably a silly enterprise. All this plotting for something so trivial. But here we are. Theo is clearly taking it seriously, which makes me think it can't be too ridiculous.

Theo isn't the kind of man to spend his time on ridiculous schemes, so maybe I'm merely feeling self-conscious about the whole situation.

"I don't remember Mick very well," I say mostly to fill the silence between us. "He played trumpet in band, didn't he?"

"Yeah. He was on the chess team with me, so I knew him better, but we never hung out much."

In my recollection, Theo didn't hang out with anyone other than Chris's circle. He and Chris were neighbors and were friends from the time they could talk. Chris was the outgoing one, and their social circle revolved around him. He pulled me into his orbit like he did everyone else. But I don't actually remember Theo having friends who weren't already in Chris's circle.

Not that I'm one to talk. I didn't either.

Maybe I still don't.

"But he'll remember who you are?"

"Yeah. Of course. We still see each other around. And I defended one of his cousins last year."

"Oh really? What was the charge? Oh, are you allowed to tell me?"

"I'm not allowed to tell you anything that falls under attorney-client privilege, but the charge is public record. He was just a kid. A couple of the guys he was hanging out with robbed a convenience store, and he was the one who was caught."

"Did you get him off?"

"Of course." He meets my eyes. "Believe it or not but I'm pretty good at my job."

"I know you are. I mean, I wouldn't have doubted it. But sometimes even good lawyers get losing cases for whatever reason."

"True. But I got Mick's cousin off. He made some less than wise choices, but he's a good kid. He didn't deserve the railroading he got."

"I'm glad you got him off then. Getting convicted for that might have ruined his life."

"I know." He's about to say more, but the front doors of the church open just then, and people start to come out.

The early service must not be very full. There are only a few dozen people filing out the doors and down the stairs after saying a few words to the priest or shaking his hand.

"Father Paul has been here a long time," I say, just an idle comment.

"Has he? I thought you went to the church down the block from Tee's."

"We do. But we visited here a few times, and I remember Father Paul from a long time ago. He was always really nice, and he made me laugh."

Our parish priest was always lofty and intimidating, so Father Paul's kind eyes and sense of humor made an impression on the sensitive little girl I used to be.

"There he is," Theo murmurs, standing up and stretching out a hand to me.

I take his hand instinctively, letting him help me to my feet. Then we wander slowly down the sidewalk toward the foot of the steps.

Father Paul sees me as we approach. He waves and grins but is waylaid by an elderly lady who is walking out slowly with a cane but obviously has a number of important insights to share with the priest.

Theo calls out for Mick, who sees him and then says something brief to his parents before stepping over to us to say hello.

"Hey, Humphrey," Mick says, shooting me a quick, casual glance. "Been a while. Do you finally have a girlfriend?"

I don't react, but Theo frowns. "This is Maya Alexander."

"Oh, Chris's girl. Right." He turns to nod at me. "Sorry about that."

"No worries. It's been a long time."

"I haven't seen you around town lately." He furrows his brow. "Have I?"

"No, I've been gone for a couple of years, ever since the car accident."

"I was really sorry to hear about that. What are you up to now?" He's obviously just being polite. He has no particular interest in talking to me, but he's going through the motions of civility.

"Maya has made an impressive name for herself on

social media," Theo puts in before I can give my normal self-deprecating response to this kind of question.

"Oh really?" Mick visibly perks up. "Are you one of those influencers? My girlfriend is trying to do that. Everything's about posting on her Instagram and TikTok. Do you have a lot of followers?"

I meet his eyes blandly. "I have a decent number, yes."

"Do you think you can maybe put in a good word for Krystal? She does all these videos of herself primping in her clothes and hair and makeup. If you have a lot, maybe you can give her a boost."

This is not the first and won't be the last time this brand of inquiry is aimed at me, and I'm practiced in dealing with it. "I'm not sure my brand will really fit hers, but I wouldn't mind giving her account a look."

I wait for a minute as Mick pulls up Instagram on his phone so he can tell me his girlfriend's handle. I make a show of jotting it down and saying I'll look through it, but I'm not sure I'll be able to help her much.

Mick appears satisfied with my gesture. He turns back to Theo and says, "Hey, thanks again for helping out Jake last year."

Theo gives an appropriate response and catches my eye with a silent question. I give my head a discreet shake.

There is absolutely no reason to go through with the questions we planned in advance for these encounters.

There's no way in the world Mick is my pen pal unless he's the most convincing actor I've ever seen.

He has no idea who I am online, and he doesn't care, except in how I might help his girlfriend. He's not the person we're looking for.

Theo reads my signal and tells Mick we've got to get going. We tell him goodbye as he returns to his parents, who were waiting for him at the foot of the steps.

"Well, that's another one we can cross off," Theo says as he takes my arm as we walk away.

I turn my head to shoot one more smile at Father Paul, who is still being monopolized by the old woman, before I look back up at Theo. "Yep. One down. Nine more to go."

Our next stop is a bistro downtown for brunch since one of our potentials is the owner and is always there on Sundays, the biggest day of the week for the restaurant.

It's crowded, of course, since it's prime time for weekend brunch. We have to wait twenty minutes to get a table and then another half hour for our food. At that point, we've still seen no sign of Jesse Angus. Theo finally asks our friendly server, who tells us that Jesse is on vacation for a week.

So our entire goal in coming here gets thrown out the window. At least the food is good. I eat most of my Belgian waffle and a section of Theo's omelet. (He offers a much bigger piece than I expect when I ask for a taste.)

Fortunately, most of the people brunching here today are the ultrawealthy in town. Not the regular wealthy of most of our social circle. So I only recognize a few people, and they don't recognize me at all.

The whole thing takes almost two hours out of our day for no purpose, but I don't have as bad a time as I would have expected. Theo has gotten less silent and scowly with me as the weekend has passed. He's still not what I would consider a chatter, but he answers questions readily and he asks a few of his own. We talk at first about our strategy for the last two potentials on our list for today. Then he asks me about some of the places I've traveled over the past two years, and that conversation takes us through the end of our meal and then almost twenty minutes after we're done eating.

It's fine. We've already planned to spend all day together—at least until we encounter and talk to everyone on our list. It's not like it matters if we're hanging out having brunch or killing time in the car, waiting for our next man to ambush.

On our way out, someone calls out to Theo, so we pause to say hello to a very handsome man and a blonde who is obviously his wife. Friendly and engaging, the man smiles at me after he greets Theo.

I might stare just a little. The man is ridiculously good-looking with the most vivid green eyes I've ever seen.

"This is Maya Alexander," Theo says, putting a hand on my back to nudge me forward slightly. It felt like his conversation, so I was standing a step farther back. "Maya, this is Lincoln and Summer Wilson."

Lincoln Wilson. That's a name I've heard before. He's several years older than us, and I don't actually remember ever seeing him in person before. He's the son of one of Green Valley's premiere families, and his wife is the only heir of a billionaire's fortune.

These are lofty circles indeed.

I expect either Lincoln or Summer to associate me with Chris—since that car accident that killed him was big news in town for months—but they don't appear to recognize my name. Lincoln asks me about myself briefly, and then he asks Theo about his work. Summer asks what we got for brunch, and the conversation ends naturally on a friendly note.

I'm absolutely certain that Lincoln and Summer came away from that conversation assuming that I am Theo's girlfriend, but he's too clueless to realize how it must have come across.

It makes me a little squirmy, but I don't mention it. Not because I'm particularly discreet or tactful but because I don't want to raise the topic at all. The next time they run into Theo, he can clarify matters to them.

What strangers believe about my relational status isn't something to worry about.

~

Our next stop is the country club, and if things go well, we can happen to run into both our final targets for the day there.

Unsurprisingly, I'm not a member of the country club. My family never was and wouldn't want to be even if we were able to keep up with the hefty annual fees. I'm actually surprised that Theo is a member since he doesn't seem to be the type, but he explains his parents gift him the membership every year. He occasionally meets acquaintances over golf, or he takes out his parents' boat from the connected marina.

I didn't realize before that his family is a country-club type. No wonder Chris's parents always encouraged their friendship when they discouraged his relationship with me.

Whatever the reason, his membership comes in handy to us today. We're able to get in to a place we otherwise wouldn't have been able to set foot in.

Billy Curtis was in Chris and Theo's year in school. Theo says he hasn't kept up with him since graduation, but he's heard he's always at the country club if he isn't at work.

We luck out this time. As soon as we check into the front desk and walk in one of the lush lounge areas in the main building, Theo nods toward a man working at a table on a laptop.

I'm not sure I would have recognized him if Theo hadn't pointed him out. He's thin and has a kind of coffeehouse aesthetic with his receding hairline and small goatee.

He's nothing I would have expected from his appearance, however. Theo greets him when we wander over in his direction, and then we both sit down in nearby chairs without waiting for an invitation.

After a few minutes of conversation, it's clear to me that Billy is not interested in friendly conversation. He's holding on to the bare minimum of courtesy, but he's more absorbed in the work he's doing on his laptop than anything either one of us has to say.

My introduction has zero effect on him. He doesn't care about me in even the slightest way. When Theo mentions that I'm a successful influencer, he does ask me if I'm interested in investing because he could help me with that. As soon as I make it clear I'm not a potential client, he loses all interest in me.

I meet Theo's eyes when Billy turns back to his laptop. There's no way this could be my pen pal. He'd never drag himself away from work enough to sustain a lengthy correspondence with someone who couldn't help him financially.

At least it didn't take long to determine that fact. We get up by mutual agreement and walk out of the lounge and down the hall toward the restaurant.

We glance in, just to be sure our final potential isn't there. When we discover he's not, we keep walking.

Theo told me that, as far as he's ever seen, Reston Graber is always here on the weekends. But the country club is huge. He could be on the tennis courts or on the golf course or in one of the social areas or down by the lake and marina.

We walk around for about twenty minutes until we spot him at one of the bars, drinking beer with a few of his friends.

He was the year between me and Theo, and he was my lab partner for a while in a biology class. I've never thought much about him, but he was always friendly enough. Surely it won't be too hard to get him talking.

While Theo goes up to get us drinks, I stroll over to a table near the one where Reston is seated. He's attractive enough with longish blond hair and a wide, white smile. When he glances in my direction, I smile and wave at him.

He looks slightly confused, but maybe that's because he's drunk too much. He glances around to make sure I'm smiling at him, and then he hefts himself up to come sit beside me.

"Hi," he says, sliding onto the bench seat right next to me. Way too close to me. He smells strongly of beer. "I know you from somewhere, beautiful, but you'll have to remind me where."

Oh great. He's like that. "We were in biology together a long time ago."

"Oh yes. Mala. Mava." He blinks several times, making great effort to think.

"Maya." I correct him with a smile, easing away from him slightly. His hand is already touching my thigh. "It's been a long time."

"Too long. Where have you been hiding yourself away?" He leans close. Very close.

I lean back as discreetly as I can. I don't want to offend him since I need to talk to him, but I really don't want him breathing on me. "I've been traveling. I'm just back in town for the holidays."

"Well, I'm glad you came back. What are you doing tonight? I can keep you company if you need—"

"Graber!" The one word cuts into the uncomfortable vibes like a knife. Theo is looming over us. "You're in my seat. Clear out."

Some people get angry when they're drunk. Some people, on the other hand, are utterly compliant. Fortunately, Reston is the latter. He obediently gets off the bench and collapses into the chair across the table from me.

Theo slides onto the bench right beside me.

It's a relief. He's close but not all over me. And he smells pleasant—like soap and laundry and coffee—not like beer.

He slides a glass of light white wine in front of me. "What have you been up to since high school, Graber?"

Reston looks annoyed and confused both. Like he's not getting something he wanted, but he can't actually remember what that was. He shrugs. "Hanging out."

His family has money. That much I remember. And he must be one of the trust-fund kids who don't work.

Not all the wealthy in Green Valley are like that, but a lot of them are.

"Are you two together?" Reston asks, still looking rather baffled by this whole encounter.

"Yes," Theo says blithely with no hesitation at all. "Sorry to disappoint, but she's not available."

I shoot him a quick look, slightly annoyed with his high-handedness but not enough to make a fuss. After all, his bristly attitude has saved me from Reston's unwanted advances.

"Too bad," he says with a sigh, wrapping his fingers around his glass of beer and standing up unsteadily. "We could have had a damn good night."

"I'll live with the disappointment," I reply.

I don't think this man can be my pen pal any more than

Billy or Mick, and I don't want to waste more time talking to him.

His name is getting crossed off my list for sure.

He reaches over toward me. I'm not exactly sure why since he's so wobbly, but it feels like he's going to touch me again, and I don't want him to. I shrink toward Theo.

"Hands off," Theo says bluntly, wrapping an arm around me.

Reston gives a little huff. "Y'all are no fun at all."

I giggle as he slouches away. Then I can't seem to stop. I turn my head and laugh against Theo's shoulder until I realize what I'm doing.

This is not how we interact at all.

I don't even like this man. Why am I snuggled all up against him?

When I straighten, he retrieves his arm, but he doesn't get up and move to the chair. He stays right beside me on the bench until we've finished our drinks.

∼

We're walking out at the same time as Reston has gotten refills of beer for him and his friends. He's loping toward us, carrying two glasses in each hand. Maybe he does it on purpose. Maybe he's really that drunk.

Either way, he doesn't steer clear of our path. And when we draw abreast of each other, he bumps into me, spilling two of the glasses all down the front of my favorite red-and-brown dress.

I let out an exclamation, and Theo barks out something to Reston about watching where he's going. The bartender points out a restroom where I can clean up, but I can only do so much.

The front of my dress is drenched, and I can smell nothing but beer.

It's almost sickening.

I'm drooping when I come out of the bathroom and walk over to where Theo is waiting for me.

"Well, this has been a messy end to an unsuccessful day."

"We were able to cross three names off your list, so it wasn't entirely unsuccessful," he says, putting a hand on my back as we start toward the door. "But I agree the end could have been better."

"Now my truck is going to smell like beer forever." I sigh, hating the idea of it. Chris was killed by a drunk driver. I wasn't around during the accident and have no idea if beer was involved, but I still haven't drunk beer since.

"We're close enough to my place to walk. You can shower and change there so the smell doesn't get into your car."

I look at him, relieved by the suggestion but wondering if he thinks I'm overreacting. After all, it's just beer. Not the end of the world. "You don't mind?"

"Of course not. Why would I? We'll head over to my place, and when you're ready, I'll walk you back to your truck."

"That's a lot of wasted time for you."

"I've got no plans for the rest of the day." He meets my eyes, and I can see he's serious. He doesn't think I'm being silly, and he doesn't mind taking the time.

"Okay. Thanks. I haven't been able to deal with the smell of beer since Chris died."

"I get it. I don't mind. Come on. Let's get out of here."

5

It's almost four in the afternoon when we get to Theo's place. I'm tired from a weird day and slightly nauseated from smelling beer for so long. It's a relief to step into his bathroom and pull off my dress.

Even my boots smell like beer. And I can't just throw those into the laundry.

Reminding myself it's not really that big a deal—things like this happen—I get into the shower and stay under the spray for longer than normal.

I even wash my hair in case it smells too. Theo uses bath soap, but it's not fancy. It smells pleasant. Exactly the way you expect soap to smell. And his shampoo is good quality but also basic. Made to tame thick hair.

I smile when I read the bottle. I always suspected he wasn't fond of his thick, wavy hair. He used to cut it really short, and now it looks like he's always fighting to keep it smooth.

His shampoo will work fine on my hair. It smells like him.

Feeling a lot better after I'm done with the shower, I dry off and pull on the old gray sweatshirt and black sweatpants he gave me to put on. I'm tall enough that the clothes aren't ridiculously long for me, but they're definitely too big. I feel kind of like a little girl in adult clothes, but it's better than smelling like beer.

I braid my hair quickly into one thick, wet plait and then come out into the living room, where Theo is sitting on a stool at his kitchen counter bar.

His face changes when he sees me. He doesn't smile, but his expression softens almost imperceptibly. "You feel better?"

"Yeah. Thanks. Sorry for the freak-out."

"That was hardly what I'd call a freak-out."

"Maybe. But still... I could have probably managed to drive home without contaminating my car."

"It would have left a smell. So this plan made more sense."

This plan really doesn't make more sense than driving home like a reasonable person, but I appreciate that he's making me feel like my behavior wasn't irrational. "Thanks for letting me use your shower and your clothes."

"Not a problem. Will your dress go in the laundry

okay? We can wash it now if you want so you don't have to take it home smelling like that."

I hesitate because I like the idea, but it will require me staying here for long enough to wash and dry it. "It will. But you really don't have to—"

He doesn't let me finish the statement. He's already picked up my dress and taken it to a closet in his hallway, which houses a small stacked washer and dryer.

I help him choose the wash settings and put in the detergent. I'm glad the dress isn't like a lot of my other clothes and requires handwashing.

"Well, now I'm stuck here for a while, unless you want me to leave before it's—"

"Are you serious, Maya?"

He sounds so baffled that I stare. "About what?"

"You really think I'm expecting you to take off before your dress is even done?"

I swallow hard. "Well, no. Probably not. But I didn't know. I've never been your favorite person."

"What do you know about who my favorite person is?"

I'm not expecting this kind of response from him. I'm used to him being grumpy and withdrawn, even when he's trying to be civil. "I... I don't know."

I expect him to back down. Drop the subject. Look away. That's what he's always done before whenever conversation between us got serious in any way.

But he doesn't this time. He's looking right at me, and he doesn't drop his gaze. "What don't you know?"

"I don't know... I mean, you can't pretend you ever really liked me. I appreciate that you've been good to me this weekend, but you've never... you've never liked me."

He pauses a beat before he asks in an oddly textured voice, "Is that what you think?"

An excited shiver runs up and down my spine. I have no idea where it even comes from. I open my mouth to reply and then close it again. Don't say anything.

We stare at each other for almost a minute—about fifty-five seconds too long. Then I finally drop my gaze and clear my throat. "Anyway, thank you."

"For what?"

"For the shower and the laundry and not acting like I'm making a big deal about nothing. And for helping me this weekend even though I'm sure you think the whole situation is ridiculous."

"Why would I think it's ridiculous?"

"Because it kind of is. Who makes a huge production over figuring out the mystery person who's been writing her?"

"If he's been writing you regularly for a year, then he must be into you. Trying to discover who it is isn't a ridiculous thing to do."

I've never actually put into words the significance of

my faithful correspondence with this person, but Theo is exactly right. The most logical explanation is that he's into me.

And the most logical explanation for my reciprocation is that I might be a little bit into him too.

That moves my mission here beyond simple curiosity and wanting to meet a challenge. And it also makes me feel very weird—because what does it say about me that I might be into a mystery man but I'm also having very weird, excited feelings about Theo?

The whole thing is awkward and bizarre and laughable. Only I could get myself into this situation.

"If he's really into me, then he wouldn't be trying to hide his identity."

"Maybe. Maybe not." He scoots the stool beside him away from the bar in a clear invitation for me to sit.

I do. "Why maybe not?"

"There might be reasons why he's reluctant to make himself known."

"Reasons like what? Other than the possibility that he's married or ninety years old or something."

He huffs with amusement. "He might be shy."

"Shy?"

"Yes. Why not?"

"He wasn't too shy to start writing to me."

"There's a difference between writing from behind a

screen and coming face-to-face. Maybe he's bad with women."

I twist my mouth. "I guess. But he doesn't seem bad with women. He's really smart and funny and sensitive."

"Online. That doesn't mean he has any sort of game in person."

"Maybe. But if that's the case, what does he hope to accomplish by the whole thing? If he's serious, then he'll have to tell me who he is eventually."

Theo stares down at the granite bar for several seconds. Then murmurs thickly, "Maybe he's been into you for a really long time and he's afraid this is his one shot with you. Maybe he's terrified of blowing it."

For some reason, my heart does a dramatic leap in my chest. I dart a couple of quick glances at him, uncertain what's causing the thick tension in the air between us.

I wait for him to say something else, partly because I have no idea what to say and partly because I'm not sure my voice is actually going to work.

Until he clears his throat. "I'm just saying, we don't know what this guy is thinking. And there's no reason to assume his motivation is dubious."

My heart returns to its normal place in my chest. "I know what you're saying, but I think your interpretation is overly romanticized."

His shoulders shake briefly, and he turns his head to

slant me an amused look. "Since when has anyone accused me of being overly romantic?"

"I'd imagine no one ever has."

"They haven't. But I still stand behind my words. You don't really know what's going on with this guy, so don't assume the worst."

"Okay." I sigh and slump forward, resting my arm on the countertop and using it to support my head. "So we're right back where we started, trying to figure out which guy on my list we're dealing with."

"But we've crossed three off."

"True."

"And we've got plenty of time to track down the others. You're here for three weeks, right?"

"Right."

"So there."

I can't help but giggle. "So there."

He pushes back his stool. "You might as well stay for dinner since we have to wait for your laundry anyway."

It's only four thirty. I wouldn't say dinner was an inevitable next item on an agenda for the day. But I'm having a better time with Theo than I ever dreamed I would. Not just because it's kind of fun being on a mission with him but also because he's making me think, making me feel things, making me feel alive in a way I haven't in a really long time.

So I say, "Okay. That makes sense."

We both nod as if my words are true.

But I'm honestly not sure any of this makes sense at all.

∼

We end up moving to the couch and finding a movie to watch on TV.

When I shiver, Theo digs up some hot chocolate packets from his cabinet and makes some for both of us. He offers me a soft throw blanket, and I cuddle up under it, sipping my hot chocolate and feeling cozy and comfortable, even with my wet hair.

We watch an old mystery film about an amateur detective following clues and solving an enigma of a case.

I enjoy every minute of it.

When the movie is over, it's six thirty, so it's well within the appropriate span of time to start fixing dinner.

He has a reasonably full refrigerator and freezer as well as a decent number of staples in his cabinets. He clearly is in the habit of cooking his meals at home somewhat often, so it's not hard to find something for dinner.

He's got some good sausage and gorgonzola, so I suggest pasta with sausage and a gorgonzola cheese sauce. He tells me I'll have to take the lead on the sauce, so he ends up making us a simple salad to eat with the pasta.

He pours us both glasses from a bottle of merlot he

pulls out of the cabinet above the refrigerator and then he turns on music while we cook.

It's a mix of older country music. It kind of surprises me, although I'm not sure I ever put any thought into what kind of music Theo might listen to.

I'm smiling to myself about the twangy love song as I add dried pasta to boiling water when he glances over at me from the grape tomatoes he's slicing in half. "What? Do you not like this music? Would you prefer some sort of mystical Zen yoga music?"

I laugh out loud. "I like the kind with forest and rain sounds interspersed."

His mouth twitches. "I thought as much. I can find you something like that if you really want."

"This is fine. Believe it or not, I don't listen to nature sounds all the time. I just never thought of you and country music."

"My grandpa used to listen to it all the time. I spent summers with him growing up, and I guess it made an impact."

"I didn't know you spent summers with your grandpa." I search my mind, trying to recall whether this particular fact was something I should have known.

"Yeah. My folks liked to travel in the summer, so they sent me to him."

"Didn't you want to travel with them?"

"Sure. I wouldn't have minded, but they never

suggested it. They preferred adult trips. And I always loved staying with Grandpa. He taught me to drive and to shoot a rifle and to camp and all kinds of outdoorsy stuff I never would have done with my folks."

I turn the sliced sausage to brown the other sides. "Where did he live?"

"In the mountains up toward Asheville. They were good summers. But that's when I learned to like this music."

"That makes sense. Is he still alive?"

"He is, but he had to move into an assisted living place a few years back. He hated it at first, but he's finally gotten used to it. It's a couple of hours away from here, but I go visit him as often as I can. At least once a month."

"I'm sure that means a lot to him. Are you closer to him than to your parents?"

His relationship with his parents is also something I never considered before. I'm realizing now that I never really thought about him as a person—just an annoying accessory to Chris. Maybe that's mostly Theo's own fault since he always kept me at arm's distance, but still...

It's also partly my fault. I could have made more of an effort. He was important to Chris. Maybe he should have been important to me too.

He makes a face as he slides the cut tomatoes to one side and works on a cucumber. "I don't know how to answer that. I don't have a bad relationship with my parents. We haven't always seen eye to eye though, and they don't approve of all my choices."

"What choices? Your career?"

He nods.

"They didn't want you to become a public defender?"

"They were fine with me going to law school, but I think they pictured some sort of ritzy partnership at an impressive law firm. They still don't really understand."

"Why did you decide to go in this direction?" I turn down the heat on the stove before I turn to look at him. "With your family's connections, you probably could have had a lucrative career."

He shrugs and glances away.

"What? Why won't you tell me?" It's odd I'm so comfortable pushing him in this. Only two days ago I never would have dreamed he'd want to open up to me or I'd expect him to.

"There's not a clear-cut reason. I just didn't want to practice law to get rich people out of trouble. I've never cared about money as much as my folks do. I... I want to do work I'm proud of, that I can see real good come out of. So this is what I chose." He's kind of mumbly and not meeting my eyes.

My heart is beating faster than it should. And it feels a little melty. And like it's momentarily too big for my chest.

I clear my throat. "Well, it's clear you are making a positive impact. I've heard from more than one person who really appreciates what you've done for your clients."

He nods and still won't meet my eyes, but it's not because he's pushing me away. It feels more like he's embarrassed by the authenticity.

Remembering my sausage before it starts to burn, I turn back to my pan, taking the sausage out and adding some butter and flour to the pan and stirring it around before adding milk.

I check the pasta, and it only needs a couple of minutes more. Theo is putting our salads together in two bowls. I'm stirring the milk into a roux when he comes over and peers at the pan over my shoulder.

"That smells really good."

"It's the sausage. It will make anything smell good."

"That sauce is thickening up really good. So you just add cheese after that?"

"Yeah. That's it."

"That's pretty easy. Why haven't I been making this before now?"

I smile down at the pan. "That's a question you'll have to answer for yourself. If that pasta is done, you can go ahead and drain it."

We work for a couple of minutes, him draining the pasta and me crumbling the gorgonzola into the sauce and then adding back the sausage. When it's ready, he pours the pasta into the pan, and I stir everything together for a minute before turning off the heat.

"Done!" I grin at him, excited about the meal and even more so that we made it together.

"That looks like the best thing I've ever eaten."

I snort. "Wait until you taste it before you make grand statements."

We serve up the pasta and eat it on stools at the bar with our salads and wine. I ask Theo more about his work, and he tells me about some of the cases he's most proud of. Then I ask him more about his family, and he asks about mine. We talk until our bowls are empty and we've finished the bottle of wine.

It's only then that I remember my dress. I never moved it from the washer to the dryer.

I run to the hallway to move it, apologizing when I come back that I let it slide.

"Why would it matter?" he asks, gazing at me with a confused smile.

"I don't know. Just that now I can't leave until it's dry."

"Do you think I was asking you to leave?"

"No. No, of course not. I just..." I take a raspy breath and stare down at my empty pasta dish. "I'm taking up your whole day."

"I told you before. I didn't have any plans for the day anyway. And I've had a better time than I would have if you weren't here."

"Really?" I give him a quick, sidelong glance to check if he's serious.

He appears to be. "Yes. Really. Do you have delusions about my having some sort of breathtaking social life?"

I can't help but laugh at that. "Well, no. If you want to know the truth. I just always assumed…"

"That I don't like you," he finishes for me. "Yes. I'm starting to understand that." He pauses. "It's not true."

"It's not?" I wish my hair was loose so I could use it to hide my face. I'm feeling ridiculously self-conscious. Shy in a way I almost never am.

"No. It's not true."

We gaze at each other for another span of time that feels just a little too long.

I swallow and slide off my stool, picking up my dishes to bring them to the sink.

He does the same. We rinse off the dishes, load the dishwasher, and then return to the couch.

We sit in silence for a minute before he says, "We can watch another movie if you want."

"Okay. That sounds good." It does. Anything to fill the tense silence. Anything other than sliding over to him and kissing him, which is what I'm currently fighting the urge to do.

He finds another old mystery—one of a similar tone to the earlier one we watched—and I snuggle under the blanket, feeling full and warm and comfortable.

Strangely safe.

And like I'm not alone.

When the dryer buzzes, I retrieve my dress and hang it up so it won't get wrinkled. But I don't put it on yet. No use doing that until the movie is over.

During the second half of the movie, the food and the warmth start to make me sleepy. I make myself focus on the screen and not let my eyes drift shut.

I don't succeed.

I fall asleep and must lean over on him in my sleep because when my eyelids flutter open the next time, I'm cuddled up under his arm, resting my head on the side of his chest. "What's happ'ning?" I mumble.

"You were asleep," Theo says, warm and soft and husky. "You don't have to wake up yet if you don't want."

"Okay." I'm sure reason and sense would speak louder in my head if I really didn't like my current position. But I do like it. I love how it feels to recline against Theo this way. I love the feel of his arm around me. I love that I can feel the warmth of his body and the way his chest rises and falls with his breathing.

I don't want to move, so I don't. I burrow into him even more.

After that, I lose track of time. I do wake up briefly when Theo is shifting positions. He's stretching out on the couch, fitting me against him and then pulling a soft throw blanket over both of us.

I don't mind. I move with him willingly. After all, this way he can wrap both his arms around me, and I like that even more.

Maybe he's sleepy too. Sleeping on the couch is a perfectly normal thing to do.

And at the moment it doesn't matter that the two of us absolutely shouldn't be doing it together.

So I go back to sleep in his arms, and it's a long time before I wake up again.

6

I SLEEP UNTIL 3:48 THE NEXT MORNING.

Even then, as soon as I open my eyes, I feel like I could use a few more hours. I'm comfortable and cozy, warmer than usual and with an odd sense of pleasure in my chest and belly. It's a safe feeling. Intimate.

It's not until I lift my head and really focus around me that I realize why.

I'm still on the couch at Theo's apartment. He's still asleep, pressed up beside me and with his arms wrapped around my body. He feels big and warm and solid and as hot as a radiator. His breathing is slow and steady, and his heart is beating beneath my ear.

And I love it.

All of it.

I feel secure. Protected. Cared for. Treasured.

It's no doubt a drastic misreading of the accidental situation. Despite his grumpy ways, Theo could simply be a snuggler by nature and I was a convenient body. There's never been anything romantic or intimate between us. Until this weekend, there's never been anything even remotely friendly.

So no matter how it feels to wake up with him holding me like this, I would be the biggest fool in the world to assume it means more.

Besides, it can't mean more.

This is Theo. Chris's best friend.

And that's an emotional ick that's impossible to overcome.

I sit up abruptly, pulling out of his arms when he instinctively tightens them. He makes a few mumbly sounds that sound disapproving.

"Too early," he says when I continue withdrawing from his embrace.

Finally I'm sitting up on the foot of the couch, hunched over and hugging my arms to my chest because I'm suddenly cold and shaky. It was so warm cuddled up with him.

But now it's not.

"I know," I manage to say. "Sorry. I need to get back home."

It takes a minute, but awareness finally penetrates the fog of sleep. He pushes himself upright and drops his legs over the edge of the couch like I did.

His hair is a mess, rumpled from sleep with pieces sticking out in all directions. He's got stubble all over his jaw and neck, the same brownish red as his hair. His eyelids are heavy, but his vivid blue eyes are sharp. Intelligent.

"You okay?" he asks, giving me a quick, sidelong glance.

"Yeah. Just kind of out of it. I didn't mean to sleep for so long."

"Me either."

That's probably true. It was an accident on both our parts. It happens, and it doesn't mean anything except we had a long day, ate a good meal, and were relaxing on the couch.

All these tumultuous, terrifying fluttery feelings expanding inside me are unnecessary and inappropriate.

I really need to pull it together.

Half my hair has slipped out of my braid as it dried, and the loose strands are hanging down on either side of my face. I drop my head so I can hide my expression behind it.

He leans over. Very gently pushes some of the hair back behind my ear. "Maya?"

"I'm fine. Sorry. Just trying to wake up."

I'm fully awake already. There's no way I could keep sleeping through this uproar in my head.

"Are you sure that's all it is? Because nothing that happened last night is—"

"Nothing happened," I choke out, cutting off his words because I'm so scared of how he might finish that sentence.

He's silent for more than a moment. Then he says, "I know that. We fell asleep."

His tone is almost imperceptibly different, but I can feel the shift. He feels cooler. More withdrawn.

And it hurts as much as anything has.

But it's safer that way. It's the only way I'm ever going to get over this emotional storm rushing through me. "Sorry to be weird." I try very hard to sound natural, and I almost succeed. "I feel all confused and discombobulated. But I really do need to get going. Claude and Ed have been by themselves since yesterday morning."

"Oh no. I didn't think about them. Are they okay on their own for so long?"

"Yeah. They have a litter box and water, but they usually get a little bedtime snack, and they won't be happy about missing out on it. Plus they're not used to me being gone for so long. I need to get back."

"I'll drive you." He's already getting up, pulling down his shirt and yanking up his trousers since they got disarrayed as he slept.

"You don't need to—"

"Yes, I do. Your truck is still at the country club, and it's not even four in the morning. You can't walk all that way on your own. I'll take you home for now, and then we'll go get your truck sometime tomorrow."

"You have to work, don't you? I'm awake enough to be fine driving home. Maybe you can just drive me to my truck if you don't mind."

It looks like he's about to object, but then he must change his mind. He gives a curt nod and a grunt that's probably acquiescence.

I go to the bathroom, using it and then changing into my dress. I leave Theo's sweats folded neatly on the sink counter.

He's ready to go when I come back, keys in his hand. We walk down to his midsized, moderately priced SUV in silence, and then—also in silence—he drives me to the country club where I parked my truck yesterday afternoon.

He gets out as I do, standing and waiting as I unlock the driver's door and climb in. I look over at him, growing more and more upset.

It's like yesterday didn't even happen. He's back to being the tense, scowly, withdrawn guy I've always known.

I don't want that guy. I want him to be the man he was yesterday.

But that's the most dangerous person he could be. To me.

"Okay. Thanks for everything yesterday."

"You're welcome," he mutters, his eyes focused on the pavement at his feet. "It was nothing. No big deal."

It didn't feel like nothing to me, but maybe it did to him. I'm the one so needy all of a sudden that I'm trying to transform a relationship that's never even been close into some sort of romance.

It can't be that.

It can never be that.

So his old, reserved, mumbly self is a better option in keeping myself out of emotional danger.

"Okay." I swallow hard. "Well."

"Drive safe back."

"I will."

"Text me when you get back."

I frown at him, confused by why he wants that.

"So I know you're back safe." He's still not meeting my eyes.

My heart does another one of those silly leaps. "Okay. See you later."

"See you."

He closes the door for me and retreats as I turn on the ignition. I can still feel his eyes on me as I back out of my parking place and drive away.

∼

At home, I'm greeted by a chorus of feline yowls as I step inside. Ed's are happy, and Claude's are reproachful. Both of them demand a snack and gobble it down quickly.

Then I change into pajamas, wash my face and brush my teeth, and climb up into my loft to flop down on my mattress.

Ed and Claude come to join me. Ed curls up right beside me for a snuggle while Claude makes a few passes, begrudgingly accepting some pets before he settles into the window nook he prefers to sleep in.

I text Theo to let him know I got home safely. Then I close my eyes eventually and try to go back to sleep.

I don't even come close to succeeding.

～

Later that morning, at around ten, I drive over to visit Tee for coffee and cinnamon bread. Daniela isn't working today until one, so she's there too. She was working in the studio but takes a break to join us at the kitchen table for a while.

We talk about Tee's bad hip and then about Daniela's bad date on Saturday night. I do my best to participate in my normal manner, but I'm exhausted and groggy and confused with an anxious ball of tension in my gut.

It doesn't take long for Tee and Daniela to notice.

After we fall into silence for a minute, Tee finally asks, "Are you going to tell us what you're so upset about?"

"I'm not that upset," I reply, blinking at her and then at my cousin. "I'm really tired."

"Why are you so tired? Did you have a busy night?" That's Daniela with her typical sharp dryness.

"No, I didn't have a busy night."

"Maria called last night and mentioned she'd heard you spent the day with that very serious young man."

There can be no doubt that the "very serious young man" at issue is Theo. I give Tee a narrow-eyed look.

"You don't have to give me that disapproving look. I wasn't gossiping. She no doubt wanted news on the topic, but I didn't give her any."

"Thank you for that," I say, the tension softening in my throat.

"So you did spend the day with Theo?" Daniela asked, looking more curious than anything else.

"Well, yeah. Kind of. But it's Tee's fault. She's the one who pressured him into helping me figure out my pen pal."

"Why would Theo know?"

"He doesn't know. But Tee thought he'd be a good person to bounce ideas off of. So he's been helping me interview my potentials."

Daniela laughs softly. "So you two have been going around conducting interviews with unsuspecting targets?"

I can't help but giggle too. It is kind of silly when you think about it that way. "It's not as ridiculous as it sounds. I mean, maybe it's a little ridiculous, but I think it's a legitimate mission. We're being discreet about it."

"And Theo also believes this to be a reasonable and rational way to spend his weekend?"

My shoulders stiffen. "Yes. I mean, maybe he was a little bit pressured by Tee, but if he thought it was too stupid, he would have said so. He's been helping me for real."

"He was good friends with Chris," Tee puts in with an odd, overly casual manner. "No doubt he feels responsibility toward Maya because of that. After all, Chris would want her to be happy, and the Humphrey boy likely feels obliged to help because of that."

This comment might make sense from a certain point of view, but it doesn't sit well with me at all. It doesn't feel right or true, and the fact that Tee is the one who spoke it is highly disorienting.

Tee is watching me with a sideways look, and Daniela is openly staring with a skeptical expression. "Is that what it is, Maya? He's feeling obliged?"

"I... I don't know."

"Don't you?" Daniela has a blunt manner that's sometimes refreshingly direct and sometimes like a punch to the gut.

"Why else would he be helping?" Tee asks, her gazing moving down to her coffee cup. "It appears he devoted his entire weekend to you. What other reason could there be than guilt and responsibility because of Chris?"

She sounds light. Innocent. Guileless.

And Tee is never innocent.

My spine stiffens even more. "If you have something to ask, you can just ask it."

"Yes. I know that. But if I asked it directly, you would never answer me."

"I would too."

"You would try, but you're in protection mode right now. No one should blame you for that. It's entirely natural and normal. But because of it, there are a number of things you don't want to admit to yourself."

The words hit me like a blow. Leave me stunned and breathless. It takes a minute for me to get even a few words said. "But... But I don't... I don't think that's..."

"Maybe not. But that's what it looks like to me." Tee's expression is gentler than normal. "I'm trying not to trap you in a corner with a host of realizations you're not ready for. But that very serious young man would not have spent his entire weekend on such a dubious enterprise out of nothing more than secondhand responsibility."

I swallow several times over a hard lump. "He... he's just helping me."

"Yes," Tee replies. "He is. But why is he helping?"

"Because he..."

I have no coherent answer to give her because there's only one answer that comes to me. Only one answer that feels right.

He must not dislike me anymore. He must have some

sort of warm feelings for me. After all, there's no other explanation for the way he held me in his arms all night.

Even if he's a covert snuggler, he wouldn't want to snuggle with a woman he doesn't even like.

My face gets warmer and warmer as I come to this conclusion. As I remember how he was holding me last night. How he acted yesterday evening. How close to him I felt.

I have to use both hands to cover my face, desperately needing to hide for a few seconds.

Hide from... everything.

"Shit," Daniela breathes. "So you and Theo are really into each other?"

"No!" The words come out loud and raspy. "No! We... we can't be."

"Why not?"

"Because..." I'm almost gasping now, so I take a minute to catch my breath. "Because we can't be. Because of Chris. It would be... weird and cringey and wrong."

"Not wrong," Tee murmurs very softly.

"I'm sure it could feel kind of awkward," Daniela says in a less gentle, more matter-of-fact voice. "I think it would to me. But it's been two years. Enough time has passed. These things happen."

"They do? Other women get feelings for their dead fiancé's best friend?"

Tee shrugs. "Of course they happen. You think you're the first woman something similar has happened to?"

"N-no. Of course not. But that doesn't make it... make it right." I rub my face, trying to clear my mind of too much emotion. "So, yeah, maybe I've picked up a few stray feelings toward Theo, but they can't go anywhere. They can't lead to anything. They can't."

"Okay," Daniela says with a shrug. "So they don't go anywhere. No big deal."

I peer at her. Then at Tee. "No arguments?"

"Why would there be arguments? You know best how you feel. And one thing has always been true about human beings. Feelings are real but they aren't always right. We are capable of doing what's right, no matter what our feelings are telling us. If you truly believe starting something with Theo is wrong, then you shouldn't do it."

"That's right," Daniela adds. "Why don't you text him and thank him for his help but that you can handle it on your own from here on out?"

I stare at her, my lips parting slightly.

"What?" she adds. "He's a sharp guy. He's going to understand what that message means. He won't make another move on you after that."

"He never made a move on me." My voice cracks slightly on the last word.

Holding me in his sleep doesn't count.

"Well, he'll know to never try anything. He'll back off."

Tee reaches over to pat my forearm, which is resting on the table. "Daniela is right. That young man is too shy to push his way in if you don't open the door for him."

"He's not—" I cut off my own claim since I'm no longer certain it's true.

Maybe he is shy. Maybe everything I always believed about Theo is completely wrong. What the hell do I know about anything anymore?

He was so sweet last night. And even this morning after we woke up—until I made it very clear that nothing was happening between us.

It was only then that he pulled back.

"Not everyone acts in the exact same way with certain traits. A lot of people who are generous channel it in ways that look different. So why would you assume people who are shy always look or act in the same ways?" Tee smiles to soften her targeted question. "Maybe you can just trust me in this."

I nod and look down at the plate on the table in front of me—nothing left on the surface but crumbs from my piece of cinnamon bread. "Okay. Maybe you're right."

"So go ahead and text him," Daniela says again, gesturing toward my phone set beside my plate. "Get it over with, and you'll feel better."

Maybe I would, but that's not how it feels right now. It feels like texting him those words—slamming the door on anything that might grow between us—would hurt as much as chopping off my hand.

"It wouldn't be wrong?" I ask in almost a whisper.

"Why exactly do you think getting with Theo would be wrong?" Daniela asks.

"I don't know. Just that Chris was the love of my life. My soulmate. You're not supposed to fall for your soulmate's best friend, are you?"

Daniela chuckles at this, but Tee gives her head a firm shake and says, "You don't really believe in soulmates, do you?"

The disapproval in her tone surprises me since she's been so gentle throughout this entire conversation. "I... I don't actually know. It was mostly a figure of speech."

"Good." She smiles, softening her tone and her expression. "Because the idea that there's only one person in the entire universe we can truly love and be happy with is appalling if you really think about it. Most of us would be wandering around lost and alone, never finding our one perfect mate. Because what is the chance that your one person in the entire universe happens to be your same town, your same school, your same church, your same circle of friends? But that's where most people end up finding the person they love."

I think about that for a minute and finally smile back at her. "I guess that's true."

"Our hearts aren't made of Daniela's marble, chiseled by force into a shape that only matches with one other person and then shatters into pieces when that matching piece is snatched away. Mija, our hearts are indeed fragile, vulnerable to being hurt. But they're *soft*. Malleable. And like clay they're also resilient. They mold themselves around other hearts, taking new shapes at different stages of life."

Her words hit me hard. My eyes burn, and my throat closes. I blink away a few tears.

"This has always been true. Our hearts adapt to circumstances. We fall in love with the people around us, whoever they are. Even possibly our dead fiancé's best friend."

A few tears slip down my face despite my best efforts.

"If you want a real mystery to solve," Tee continues, reaching over to squeeze my hand, "then I present to you the mystery of the human heart. Broken and remade a hundred times in a lifetime. Ever seeking to love and be loved."

Before I can respond to these words that cover my own heart like a cloak—warm and heavy and true—my phone vibrates on the table, the buzzing and the motion making me jerk and gasp.

I grab for it and read the screen. It's Theo.

Hey, just checking in after last night. Is everything all right between us? If you still want me to help with your mystery, I'll be done with work by six. We may be able to catch a couple of them this evening. Just let me know.

I stare at the words for a long time, reading them once and then again and again.

"It's him, isn't it?" Daniela asks.

"Y-yeah."

"Is he asking about seeing you again?" Tee asks that question.

"About... about helping more with my list of potentials. He wants to know if everything is okay and, if so, he can help me this evening after work."

"Well," Tee says with a smile, patting my arm again. "It's just as I said. He's a thoughtful, kindhearted man and not a pushy or clueless one. He's making it easy for you to tell him you're fine on your own if that's really what you want to tell him."

I gulp. Look at Tee and then Daniela and then back at my phone.

"You don't have to tell him that, if you don't want," Daniela adds.

"But... but..."

"But what? You're not announcing that you're ready to marry him or something. You're not even accepting a date. If you're not sure about shutting him down, then just see him again tonight. Stop acting like right in this moment you're having to decide the entire course of your life."

Daniela's wry voice is like a lifeline. I mentally grasp for it, holding the words in my mind as I process them.

"She's right. You don't know what you want yet, so why put up a brick wall? You can see him again tonight and see how you feel. You can end it then if you decide that's best, or you can see him again. You don't need to burden yourself with the weight of huge decisions right now. Did you have a good day yesterday?"

I very slowly nod. I had the best day I've had in a really long time.

"Then don't close him down. Not yet. See how it goes tonight."

Clearing my throat, I pick up my phone and pull up the text conversation with Theo. I start typing. Stop. Start again.

"He's going to see you keep changing your mind," Daniela comments blandly.

She's right. I'm making a huge deal about something that isn't one. Or that doesn't have to be.

After all, I'm committing to nothing right now.

Nothing.

Sorry if I was weird and awkward this morning. Everything's fine. I had a good time yesterday and really appreciate your help. I'll be happy for your help tonight too, but don't go out of your way or anything.

There. Not the most graceful of responses but it sounds

nice and genuine but basically causal. I hit Send before I can second-guess myself.

I see the three dots on the screen indicating he's responding almost immediately.

I want to help, and it's not out of my way. Greg is usually at the gym after work, and Vince sometimes is as well. We can try there first if that sounds okay?

That sounds good.

I'll pick you up at 6:15.

Great, thanks!

When I look up, both Tee and Daniela are watching me with varying degrees of smiles on their faces. "Am I really that amusing?"

Tee leans over so she can give me a one-armed hug. "We're not laughing at you, mija. We're really proud of you."

7

THEO PULLS UP BESIDE MY TINY HOUSE AT EXACTLY 6:14 THAT evening.

I've been watching for him at my front window, so I step out onto the deck as he parks and gets out. I fussed for way too long over what to wear. He said he'll be coming straight from work and will change into workout clothes at the fancy health club at the Green Valley country club, so I'm wearing regular clothes and will change at the gym too. A soft, thick green sweater dress that is cozy rather than particularly flattering and my favorite boots.

After much debate, I decided to keep it purposefully casual so that it doesn't look like I'm expecting a date.

Theo is smiling as he walks around his car to stand at the steps up to my deck, handsome and rumpled in a dark gray suit—slightly wrinkled from a day of working—and a dark red tie. His eyes run from my face to my boots and back up. "You look really nice."

My cheeks get hot. I was trying so hard to not make this feel like a date, but now it definitely does. "Thanks. I'm all ready." I've got a bag hooked over my arm.

"Can I meet Claude and Ed?" he asks, coming up the steps to stand beside me.

When I say my deck is small, I mean it's *tiny*. With both of us standing here, there are only a few inches between our bodies. My breath catches in my throat. "Sure."

I brush up against him as I turn back toward the door. He's only a few inches taller than my five-nine, but he feels a lot bigger somehow. His shoulders are broad, and his body seems to generate heat. It makes me want to snuggle up against him.

I resist the impulse.

Claude and Ed are at our feet as we come inside and delighted by this unexpected reprieve from heartless abandonment. Theo leans over to pet Ed, who promptly rolls onto his side and stretches out to better enjoy the attention. Claude, predictably contrary, keeps himself just out of reach, walking suspicious circles around Theo to assess his intentions and quality.

Theo crouches all the way down into a squat, grinning at Ed and avoiding making direct eye contract with Claude.

Maybe it's accidental and he's simply focusing on the

friendlier cat, but the show of respect works on Claude anyway. Slowly his circles tighten, getting closer and closer until he's rubbing against Theo's side.

Theo gently reaches over to scratch the cat's ears. "Thank you. I was wanting to say hello to you, so I appreciate you letting me."

Claude gives a deep, approving purr and then climbs in a series of graceful leaps onto the high shelf where he likes to perch.

I smile up at him. "He doesn't like a lot of pets like Ed does, but you got his mark of approval."

"Did I?" Theo is still smiling as he shifts his gaze up to me. "He strikes me as a hard sell."

"He is," I reply, unable to keep from smiling back. "Unlike Ed, who would gladly trade me for the first stranger who passes by with treats and pets."

"That's not true, is it, buddy?" Theo is still running his hand back and forth across Ed's thick fur. "You love Maya the best, don't you? Of course you do. And why wouldn't you? She's your person."

Ed meows in pleased agreement.

I'll admit it. My smile gets rather sappy as I witness this interaction. Part of me wants to withdraw like Claude and get some distance from the feelings, but I don't. Tee and Daniela are right. There's no reason to run away from this.

After all, it's not like Theo and I are even dating. Absolutely nothing romantic has occurred between us. Falling asleep together on the couch doesn't count.

"I didn't take you for a cat person," I say at last.

"I'm not." Theo stands up, his eyes resting on me for the first time since we came inside. "At least, I've never known myself to be. I've always liked animals though. All animals."

"Your family had a dog, didn't they?"

"Yes. I love dogs, but I love cats too. Does it have to be either dogs or cats and not both?"

"No. Of course not. But sometimes it is."

He scans the interior of my house, taking in the small kitchen, the compact living area, and the lofted bed.

"Well?" I prompt at last. "What do you think?"

"I like it. There's more room than I was expecting for the square footage. It would be a tight squeeze for a family, but for one person, it definitely works."

"Yeah. It's worked very well for me."

Ed is not pleased by Theo's wavering attention. He sits at his feet and yowls up at him.

Theo chuckles. "I guess being named after artists accounts for your volatile artistic temperament."

"Ed isn't really volatile. He just doesn't understand not getting attention when—" I break off my comment as I process what Theo said. "How did you know they're named after artists?"

I'm positive I never mentioned that to him.

"Just a guess. I thought Claude was an unusual name, but then I thought about Monet, and that seemed to fit. Ed was harder, but I thought maybe Degas." His eyebrows arch with an implicit question.

"Yes. It's Edgar. Degas. That's some good guessing."

It makes me want to hug myself and hide my face at the same time. I don't even know why. Theo is a smart guy and he's probably good at solving puzzles. There's no reason to assume his deduction has anything to do with knowledge of or attachment to me.

"Well," I say with a nervous throat-clearing. "Should we head out?"

"Yeah. Greg usually finishes up around seven, so we don't want to miss him."

I split a treat between Claude and Ed to make up for our abrupt departure, and then we head for Theo's car.

He takes my arm to help me down the steps, and the small gesture makes me shiver.

It's silly. I'm perfectly capable of walking down these steps. I do it several times a day. But Theo's unconsciously considerate gesture—like it's second nature for him to go out of his way to help and protect me—really gets to me.

I'm still trying to shake it off on the drive to the gym.

"You okay?" he asks as he pulls into the health club parking lot.

"Of course. Why?"

He shrugs. "I don't know. If you're uncomfortable about anything, you can tell me."

His words are vague enough to not corner me, but I know what he's saying. I *know* it.

I want to respond to what he's really asking me without baring myself completely, so I take a minute to think first. "I'm..." I lick my lips. "I'm all right. Really. It's hard. Sometimes. Getting back into... into life. After Chris."

I stare down at my hands in my lap, wondering if I said too much after all.

"I know it is," Theo says, a thick texture in his voice that's not normally there. "I know."

He's parked the car now. We sit for a minute in silence.

I can hear him breathe. I can hear my own slightly ragged breaths.

"I'm not expect—" Theo cuts himself off like he's rethinking his words. "There's no rush. For anything."

I swallow hard and smile up at him, understanding what he's saying and why he's saying it and appreciating it more than I can currently express. Instead, I say in a different tone, "There's no rush for anything except getting into the gym before Greg decides to head home."

Theo gives a huff of amusement and appears to shake himself up. "Exactly right. We should get moving."

Theo is a member of the country club and thus this health club, so he signs me in as a guest. From the way the staff greets him, he must come to work out here somewhat regularly.

I don't know why that surprises me. He's not some sort of bodybuilder or underwear model, but he's in good shape. His frame is large, and his body is fit and efficient.

I like it. I like how he looks and how he feels when I touch him. I like that he's strong but not flawlessly molded. I like everything about him, and I'm not sure how I went so many years without noticing how attracted I am to him.

My attraction gets more obvious when he comes out wearing gym shorts and a T-shirt. It's obvious this man will look good to me with or without clothes.

I've changed into workout clothes too—not nearly as formfitting as a lot of the women here. Not because I'm particularly modest but because it's simply not my style.

Theo is eyeing me the way I've been eyeing him. Covertly. Not gawking or leering.

And I'm hit with a surreal awareness. I can't believe I'm doing this. Feeling this way. Going through this little dance.

With Theo Humphrey.

Daniela's voice in my head, telling me not to overreact, is the only thing that keeps me from running. I'm nervous as we walk into the large room filled with workout equipment.

There are a lot of people here. It takes a while for me to sort through faces.

"There's Greg. Running on a treadmill. He always does that at the end of his workout."

I glance over in the direction Theo indicated. "Okay. Well, we should go try to catch him now before he finishes up."

"Yeah."

We start walking through what feels like an obstacle course of bodies and machines. After a minute, I realize Theo is no longer beside me.

I turn to discover he's paused to talk to someone.

To talk to a woman. A very attractive blonde in a skimpy outfit—the kind I would feel foolish wearing but that looks perfect on her.

She's smiling. She clearly likes Theo.

And as far as I can tell he likes her too.

Well, isn't that nice for them?

The surge of jealousy and possessiveness is like nothing I've ever felt before. I never even experienced it with Chris. Maybe because I was always utterly confident of Chris's regard, when I'm nothing of the kind with Theo.

Theo isn't mine. There have been some preliminary feelings, but we aren't even dating. He has every right to talk to and appreciate and even go out with another woman.

Even this pretty blonde.

No one is doing anything wrong here. Not the woman—who has every reason to flirt with a guy as great as Theo. And not Theo—who owes me absolutely nothing.

Only me. For being so ridiculously jealous over him.

I make myself swallow it down and keep walking toward the treadmills. My feelings might be irrational and petty, but I don't have to act on them.

I recognize Greg from high school. He's a tall, lanky guy with dark hair and a crooked smile. He always liked gaming and anime and weird synth music. We were never close, but he was always nice to me. I smile at him as I approach and climb on the treadmill between him and the wall.

"Maya," he says, grinning as he recognizes me. "I haven't seen you in ages. Are you a member here?"

"No. I'm just in town for the holidays." I don't mention Theo. He's still talking to the blonde. I stare down at the control panel and am immediately stumped. It's a fancy machine with complicated controls, and I have absolutely no idea how to make it go.

I'm not a gym person. My exercise consists of some light yoga and walking for however long I'm in the mood for. I might as well be trying to operate a fighter jet.

Shit, I need Theo, and he's forgotten I exist.

Greg slows down from his jog so he can reach over and power my treadmill on. "If you just want a basic walk or run, you can just use this here." He gets my machine going and shows me how to set it at a moderate pace to start out with.

"Thank you." I smile at him with genuine appreciation. "I usually just walk outside, but the weather in December isn't always amenable to that, so I figured I'd try this."

"They're always upgrading the equipment here. This is Green Valley after all."

I know exactly what he means. The wealthy population here will only be satisfied with the latest and greatest—even for their workouts.

"It always takes me a while to get used to them every time they change them."

Greg has a laid-back, easy manner I like. I'm no longer embarrassed by my incompetence.

I glance over to Theo and discover he's finally remembered that I'm here with him and he's supposed to be helping me solve my mystery. He's frowning slightly with a grumpy expression I haven't seen for a while as he peers at me walking on the treadmill next to Greg's.

What did he think I'd do? Linger submissively at his heels while he had a conversation with someone else? Wait patiently for him to deign to notice my presence?

I turn back toward Greg with another smile. "I'm not sure I've seen you since high school. What have you been up to?"

"Working with my dad, exactly as was planned for me since the cradle."

I have to think back to remember his father's business. "Oh, he sells boats, doesn't he?"

"Yes. And now I do too."

Theo has joined us at last. He's mounting the treadmill on the other side of Greg.

Giving him only a brief glance, I focus again on Greg. "I thought you might have wanted to do something more creative."

"Yeah." Greg sighs. "But what we want and what life gives us are rarely the same."

There's a poignance in his words that feels familiar to me. It hits home. "I'm sorry. That's so true. So you can't tell your dad you'd rather do something else?"

"I guess I could have. But it would have blown a hole into the family, and I wasn't prepared to do that." He shrugs. "It's fine. It is what it is. And what kind of ass would I be if I whined about being given a fairly easy position that pays a lot of money?"

"I don't know. Money changes things, but it isn't always the most important thing. I think you're allowed to whine a little if you want."

"Thanks. What have you been doing since Chris— Oh wait, someone said you've gotten big on Instagram. You travel around in a camper?"

"A tiny house. But yes, I've been taking it all over the country. I got lucky with followers, and my living expenses are pretty low, so I've been doing okay for myself these past two years."

"Oh that's good to hear. I'm really sorry about Chris. I always liked him. He was a great guy."

I gulp over a tightness in my throat, but the grief doesn't overwhelm me like it used to. "Thank you." I look past Greg to Theo, whose frown is even deeper now. "Theo let me come today as a guest."

Greg turns toward Theo as if he only now noticed he was there. "Yeah, how're you doing, man?"

"Not bad."

"Don't you normally work out in the mornings?"

"Yes, but my schedule today got turned around. Plus Maya wanted to come."

He sounds relaxed and believable. There's no way Greg is going to suspect we have ulterior motives for being here.

"I'm glad you did," he says, smiling at me again.

I smile back. "Me too."

Theo scowls.

"I've got to finish up my workout," Greg says in a different tone. "But maybe we can get together sometime while you're in town to catch up."

It feels like Theo is bristling, but I don't care. If he can chat it up with the pretty blonde, then I can meet up with Greg.

We're not together. We're not even on a date.

No matter how it initially felt like one.

"Sure, maybe we can."

This appears to satisfy Greg. He picks up the speed of his jogging to a moderately fast run. My guess from the way he's staring at the control panel is that he's trying to reach a certain distance or time before he stops.

I keep up my semifast walking, not even out of breath yet. I don't want to get all hot and sweaty, so I'm not planning to push myself too hard.

Theo started out with a slow jog, but he's speeding up now too. In fact, he's speeding up a lot.

After a couple of minutes, I glance over and see that he's keeping pace with Greg.

Nope, now he's going even faster.

As I watch, Greg starts to accelerate. He's slanting his eyes over at Theo's machine, and I realize he's checking Theo's speed on the display. He runs faster until he's matching it. Then beating it.

My lips part. I really can't believe this. Are they actually trying to race each other? Competing in some sort of macho showdown?

In a few more minutes, my suspicions are confirmed. Theo has increased his speed so he's running faster than Greg's new one. He's flushed and damp with perspiration now. He's really booking it.

What the hell? What has gotten into him? I don't know Greg well enough to guess whether this is typical for him, but he's always seemed so laid-back. And Theo has never been like this. He's never fought for the top rung on the obnoxious machismo ladder.

They've both lost their minds.

It continues for about twenty minutes, and neither one of them will back down. Finally my patience evaporates. I say in a mild, friendly tone, "Well, that's it on the treadmill for me. Theo, are you going to keep at it, or do you want to come do something else with me?"

Theo slows down immediately. Huffs, "Give me a couple of minutes to cool down, and then I'll be ready."

I give him a narrow-eyed, significant look as I climb off the treadmill. "It was good to see you, Greg. Hopefully I'll see you around."

"I'll call you," he says breathlessly with a wave, adjusting his controls to slow down his speed now too. "You really look great, Maya. I'm glad you're doing so well."

I wave back at him as I walk away. I find a bench in a corner and sit on it as I wait for Theo to finish cooling down.

When he finally joins me, I shake my head at him.

"What?" He's still breathless. Such a long sprint at those speeds can't have been easy.

"You know what. Have you seen Vince around here anywhere?"

Theo has shaken off whatever came over him on the treadmill and is his normal self again. "Yeah, I saw him come in a few minutes ago. He's over there."

"Okay. We'll try to talk to him. But no alpha-male showdown this time."

"This is a gym," Theo says, putting a hand on the small of my back as we start walking. "This place is rife with alpha-male showdowns."

"No wonder I don't like it here."

∽

We are able to catch Vince and have a four-minute conversation, but he apparently has a serious girlfriend and shows absolutely no interest in me, so I mentally cross him off the list.

So far, we've talked to more than half our list, and Greg is the only possibility for my pen pal.

The truth is I don't care that much anymore. It would be nice to know who has been writing me for the past year. I really like him and feel like there might be potential.

But there's more potential with someone else. Someone right beside me. Face-to-face. Not hiding behind a screen.

If I have to choose between Theo and an unknown correspondent, I'm going to choose Theo.

No question.

Even if I'm still kind of annoyed by his stunt on the treadmill.

We've both showered and changed into our street

clothes before we leave the club and get back in his car. I haven't exerted myself all that much, but Theo has. He's still slightly flushed.

Unlike me, he's got reddish hair and a skin tone that flushes easily. I think he's kind of cute all red in the face like this.

Not that I would dream of telling him.

"Well, we can eliminate Vince but not Greg," I say as he starts the car.

"I guess. I didn't see much chance of it being Greg."

"Why not? He fits all the characteristics, and he seemed to like talking to me. He even suggested we get together."

"Maybe."

I frown at him. "You're just annoyed because you couldn't best him in that dumb race."

"It wasn't a race. But I did best him. I was just as fast as him without any sort of warm-up."

Rolling my eyes, I say, "So you claim it wasn't a race, but you know exactly how fast he was going. Uh-huh. When do men stop being little boys?"

"Why aren't you annoyed with Greg too? He was doing the same thing."

"I know he was. But it felt like more your fault than his. You started it."

"I don't think I did. Besides, how would you even know

who started it? You weren't paying any attention to me since you were caught up in his spell."

I gasp. "I wasn't caught up in anyone's spell! I was having a regular conversation with the man. But if we want to talk about being too distracted to follow through with our plan, let's talk about you and that woman."

"What woman?"

"The woman you dropped everything to talk to for a ridiculously long time when you were supposed to be helping me."

He blinks, as if he's taken by surprise. "You mean Deanna?"

"I don't know her name, but she was the only pretty blonde you talked to this evening."

He shifted into reverse to pull out of the parking space, but now he shifts back into park, turning in his seat to face me. "That wasn't anything. She came over to say hi. What was I supposed to do?"

"You weren't supposed to do anything. I'm just saying you don't have a leg to stand on in terms of being too distracted to notice things."

He's still staring at me. Confused and still surprised and also something that looks a lot like excitement. "Are you jealous?"

My spine stiffens. "Of course not. I'm never jealous."

"Really?"

"Yes, really. And there's nothing to be jealous about here."

"Are you serious? Why the hell do you think I got into that alpha-male showdown with Greg just now? You think I wasn't jealous too?"

My face has grown hot now. I stare down at my clenched hands. "I'm not a jealous person. I've never been that way." I sniff. "I'd like to drop the subject now."

"Okay." He's relaxed from his bristles. In fact, he might actually be hiding a smile as he puts the car back into reverse, pulls out of the parking spot, and then drives out of the lot and onto the street. "Do you want to get something to eat?"

"What?"

"Eat? Are you hungry? I haven't had dinner yet, and I just ran a race."

"I thought you said it wasn't a race!"

"I was lying to preserve my dignity. It was definitely a race, and I won it." He's grinning for real now. It makes my heart melt in a seriously unnerving way. "So do you want to get something to eat?"

"I guess that would be okay."

I thought when he suggested food, he meant we'd grab something quick on the way, but he takes me to a little downtown café that must be new because I have no memory of it.

It's a cute place, and we get a private table in the far corner. I get a salad topped with all kinds of yummy stuff, and Theo gets a chicken sandwich. We talk about the men remaining on my list. Then we talk about our families and about Chris and about all kinds of fun times we remember from school.

We stay there for almost two hours, and I can't believe it's so late when the server gives us a hint that they're going to be closing soon.

We only get a few steps out the door before I realize I forgot my gloves, so Theo goes to retrieve them.

The night is cool and crisp but not cold. When Theo suggests we walk around, I have no reason to say no. The Christmas lights are all illuminated, and the mood is festive.

Theo offers me his arm as we step down a particularly high curb, and then he doesn't pull it away, so we end up walking with my hand hooked on his arm.

I like that too.

I like everything about this evening, including his ludicrous macho display on the treadmills.

He's not normally that way, so he never would have done it unless he'd felt somehow like Greg might be a threat.

Exactly the way I felt with Deanna.

We wander for an hour, talking occasionally but about nothing deep or serious. It's almost ten thirty when we finally return to the car.

He comes with me to open the passenger door for me. Then he stands right in front of me, gazing down.

It's dark, but I can see his face in the streetlights. His expression is focused, as it usually is. But also something like... tender.

I swallow hard.

"Maya," he murmurs.

A shiver runs down my spine. "Y-yes."

He tilts his head down. "Maya."

"Yes."

"Tell me no," he says very softly, leaning farther until his mouth is only an inch away from mine.

"Yes," I whisper, stretching up toward him.

I can't help it. I want this—*him*—so much.

He closes the distance between us, brushing his lips against mine very gently. It evokes such a shudder of pleasure inside me that I make a little sound and reach up to grab his shoulders.

He draws back, looks at me, then kisses me again. Deeper and more intentional this time.

It feels so good, so much like everything I want, that I grab for it eagerly. I wind my arms around his neck and kiss him back with shameless enthusiasm. Our lips move together. Then I slide my tongue into his mouth so I can play with his. I'm filled with so many sensations that I can't help pressing the whole length of my body against his so I can feel all of him I possibly can.

After a few minutes, Theo starts smiling into the kiss.

"What?" I ask, pressing a few last kisses against his mouth before I pull back.

"What, what?"

"You were smiling."

"I was happy to be kissing you."

"Oh." I drop my eyes but have to slant them up again to check his expression.

He's still warm and smiling and tender—everything Theo has always been but I never recognized before.

"I don't.... I don't know what it means," I say, suddenly getting nervous.

"You don't have to know. It was a kiss. That's all it has to be." He sounds casual, and he still looks happy, so there's no way to believe he's disappointed by what I told him.

So I smile back. Then I climb into the passenger seat and let him close the door for me.

He drives me back home, and he thanks me for the evening. He gives me a short, sweet kiss at my door, but he doesn't ask to come in, so I don't have to decide on whether or not I want that.

I'm bewildered and giddy both as I step inside to greet Ed and Claude.

It was a strange night but a good one.

I have no complaints.

8

It's been two days since I've sent a message to my pen pal, and the next morning I sit down to pull up his last message with an odd, heavy sense of guilt.

The feeling is ridiculous. I have nothing to feel guilty about. I don't even know who this man is.

But I've spent a long time—nearly a year—talking and sharing and debating with him on topics ranging from our first kisses to world politics. I've developed a relationship with him even though it's all been online.

And now I'm going to have to pull back.

Not entirely but not insignificantly.

It doesn't feel like I can continue as I've been with this man while I'm pursuing whatever this thing is with Theo.

It's hard. Unexpectedly wrenching. But I know it's the right thing to do.

Last night, he sent me a quick message. *Hey, just*

checking in. Everything all right? I haven't heard from you in a couple of days. Hope all is well.

It's a thoughtful message. Neither pushy nor presumptuous given the nature of our correspondence. I would have found it strange if he hadn't followed up.

So I need to send him a response this morning, and it takes a long time for me to compose the message. *Sorry it took me so long to get back to you. I've had some relationship stuff going on, and I think I need to focus on that right now. I'm not going to disappear on you, but we'll need to slow down a lot. I'm really sorry to do this so abruptly. You'll never know how much you've meant to me over the past year, but I can't split my heart in two. I pray you find your heart's desire waiting for you where you least expect it—this Christmas or sometime very soon.*

I'm crying by the time I've tapped out the final word, and I hit Send before I can second-guess myself.

After I blow my nose and wipe my face, I look back at my screen. He must be online checking messages right now because a response comes while I'm still sniffing.

I understand.

After a few more seconds, another line appears. *I hope you find what you're looking for, and I hope you're able to give yourself permission to do it without holding back.*

I start crying again, and when the third message comes through, I'm full-on bawling.

I never told you this before, but the first time I saw you was back in middle school. I think you'd recently moved in with your Tee and so you didn't know anyone yet. You were sitting on the brick wall outside school with your sketch pad all alone. Your hair was loose and falling all over you, and the sun was shining on it. You were the prettiest girl I ever saw in my life. I stood and stared, and maybe you sensed it because you glanced up and saw me. You smiled at me. It didn't mean anything to you. You started drawing again and forgot about me. But I never forgot it. I never forgot you and your smile and your warm, vibrant heart. I've carried them with me through life. And no matter what else happens, I'll keep carrying them with me always—along with everything we've shared this past year.

I'm not telling you this to make you feel guilty but so you'll understand how much this year has meant to me. I need for you to be happy. You were happy with Chris, and that was enough for me. I want you to be happy again—whatever that looks like and no matter who it's with. So when life gets hard and it feels like you're alone with it, please know that you're not. I'm always going to be here silently holding you in my heart.

I've completely fallen apart by the time I've read the message twice. I search my memory for the moment he described—me smiling at a boy in middle school—but I simply can't remember it. So much of that first year after my parents died and I moved in with Tee is a blur. There was too much grief. Too much fear and confusion.

But he must have been in my grade or a couple of years above it if we were in middle school together.

It's what I suspected, and it's clear now he's not going to tell me.

Not unless I'm ready to commit to something beyond an online correspondence. And I'm not. No matter how much these words have moved me, I also have Theo waiting. And he's known. Real. Warm and strong and solid. He might not be as good with words as my pen pal, but that's not the most important thing in the long run.

Theo is who I want.

For some reason, this morning has confirmed that realization in my head and in my heart. Maybe it's a little strange that he was Chris's best friend, but even that doesn't matter as much as everything else.

I lost Chris, but I deserve to be happy. And I can see myself being happy with Theo.

When I've mopped my face again, I send a text to Theo. *Are you busy tonight? You can come to dinner if you want. Or another night if it works better.*

He answers immediately. *Tonight is great. Just tell me what time.*

∼

Theo shows up at my front door that evening at exactly 6:59. He's wearing jeans and a brown V-neck sweater over a white T-shirt, and he's giving me a wide, sheepish smile. He's holding a bottle of red wine and a small red-and-white amaryllis in the cutest pot made to look like a Christmas gift.

I melt a little at the sight of him. And am even more certain that I've made the right decision. I can't imagine wanting anyone else as much as I want this big, shy, warm-hearted man.

He's definitely in a good mood today. I can sense some sort of excitement shuddering beneath the surface of his relaxed, considerate manner.

I'm excited too. And his mood makes me even more so.

My kitchen isn't large enough for major culinary productions, so I've made a variation of Tee's posole in my slow cooker and baked some corn muffins as well as some simple chocolate cookies for dessert.

We drink the wine with our meal, and everything turns out perfectly. Theo enjoys it so much he has a second helping, and I experience the oddest kind of satisfaction at making him food he loves so much.

When we're done, he helps me clean up and wash the dishes. Then we lounge together on my small couch and listen to music—one of my playlists of songs I've categorized as pleasant but not demanding full attention.

Theo reaches over to put an arm around me and pull me against him. I lean on him, feeling fond and cozy and not nervous at all.

We talked a lot over dinner, but the conversation has sunk into an easy lull. Rubbing my cheek against his soft sweater, I hear myself asking, "Do you remember the first time you saw me?"

I know why I'm asking, and it's not because I'm trying to make it a competition with the romantic confessions of my pen pal. I simply want to know.

Theo has been idly stroking my hair, which is falling loose all over my back, but his hand grows still at my question. "Why?"

"I don't know. I was just thinking about it. We've known each other a long time."

"We have. But for a long time you were Chris's girl, so I couldn't..."

"I know." I shift my position so I can peek up at his face. "Did you want to? Do... anything? Back then?"

He meets my eyes. Hesitant but not hiding. "I couldn't let myself think about it. It would have been a betrayal of Chris."

"Of course it would. I'm sorry. I wasn't implying you'd ever have made a play for me or anything. I guess I'm wondering if this is entirely new for you or if you ever had any stray thoughts before."

He swallows so hard I can see it in his throat. "I did. Have stray thoughts. But when you were with Chris, I didn't let myself indulge them. But I've always thought you were... beautiful and incredibly kind and full of... of life."

My face works at the surge of emotion. "You did?"

"Of course I did." He cups one of my cheeks with his warm hand. "Who wouldn't?"

"Well, in my experience, most men think I'm kind of weird and eccentric."

"Only if they're boring buffoons with no imagination."

That makes me giggle. I bury my face in his sweater, and he wraps both arms around me in a hug. He doesn't let go, so I adjust to get more comfortable, nudging him until he stretches his legs out the length of the couch. We end up snuggled together like that night we fell asleep with me basically lying on top of him.

It's more comforting than sexy, although I'm quite sure it wouldn't take much for me get going in that direction.

He's playing with my hair again, and I'm nuzzling the curve between his neck and shoulder. I like the scratchy texture of his jaw. I like the firm contours of his arms under his clothes. I like how much bigger he feels than me.

"We can do some more investigating this week if you want," Theo murmurs after a few more minutes of cuddling.

"What?" I've been focused so much on him I don't immediately know what he's talking about.

"Your list? Of potential pen pals? You do want to keep solving your mystery, don't you?"

I lift my head. Meet his eyes even though I warm with self-consciousness. "I... don't know."

"You don't want to?"

I clear my throat. "I... I told him..." I trail off not because I need to keep this private but because I'm not sure how Theo is going to react. Maybe it will be too much. Too serious this early in our developing relationship.

Guys get scared off easily. At least in my experience.

And I really don't want to scare Theo off.

"What did you tell him, Maya?" He brushes his knuckles along my cheekbone very gently. "You can tell me."

"This morning I told him I needed to... to pull back. On our messages. It didn't feel right. To keep talking to him when... when..."

"Because of me?" he murmurs thickly.

I nod, still propping myself above him so I can see his face. "I'm not assuming anything! I know we're still figuring things out. But it didn't feel right to..."

His mouth softens into a smile. "I understand. Thank you."

"For what?"

"For taking us seriously. I was hoping you would." He raises his other arm so he can hold my head in both his hands. "Because I'm as serious about you as I can get."

The wave of pleasure and security that washes over me is like nothing I've ever experienced before. It fills me. Consumes me. I lower my face so I can kiss him, and it gets hot and heavy almost immediately as I deepen the kiss with my tongue and rub my lower body against his.

I'm into it with my heart as much as my body, and the emotions grow with my physical arousal. I'm eager and passionate as I give myself over to the kiss, and I know Theo is with me. His body gets hot. I can feel a bulge at the front of his jeans as he grows erect. His hands are moving all over my body, sliding from my head to my back to my bottom. I'm wearing leggings with a loose tunic top, so there's only thin fabric between his hands and my skin.

Everywhere he touches burns with pleasure. I keep making hungry sounds as we kiss that would be embarrassing if I could think of such things at the moment.

He's got his hands cupped around the curve where my butt meets the back of my thighs, and he's holding it possessively as he gives a soft, guttural moan. I push up his sweater and T-shirt so I can feel his abdomen beneath it. His stomach isn't perfectly flat, and I love it. Slightly soft. Real and natural and human.

I'm getting so excited that I can't help but explore even farther. I reach between our bodies so I can feel the front of his jeans. Apply pressure to the bulge there.

He grunts and arches up slightly. Then his hold on me shifts and he gently eases me up, breaking the kiss. "Maya. Maya, hold on a minute."

The abrupt end to the embrace is like a blow. I blink and pant and try to make my mind work. "You don't want me like that?"

"Of course I want you like that!" His face twists in

obvious effort to restrain himself. "Maya, sweetheart, I'm dying to be with you like that. But... But maybe we should take it a little slower."

I've somehow ended up between his legs. I shift my knees on the sofa to withdraw a few inches so I'm not resting my weight against his groin. "You want to go slow?"

"I don't want to, but I think maybe we should. This has been fast. Less than a week. And I'd like to be sure..." He works his jaw and glances away from me. "I'd like to be sure this is really what you want—and that you're ready for it—before we have sex."

I understand what he's saying, and from a certain perspective, it makes sense. But my whole body is pulsing with desire for him, and I want him now. "It feels like I'm ready. I know it's fast, but sometimes you just... just know."

"I hope so." He gives me a little smile. "You're a spontaneous, passionate person, and I love that about you. But I'm... I'm not. I've been living with this for a long time, and I'd rather give us a little breathing room to... to settle into being together. The last thing I want is for you to have sex with me impulsively and then regret it. I don't think I can live with that."

I understand exactly what he's saying and why he's saying it. He's right. Not that I can imagine regretting sex with him—I can't remember ever being so sure about anything—but I have had moments in the past where I jumped in headfirst and then had to live with the consequences.

He wants to be careful, and that's not wrong.

He might even be right.

So I nod and start to sit up. "Okay. That's probably a good idea."

"Where are you going?" he demands, grabbing me so I can't pull away from him.

Confused, I hold myself halfway up and frown down at him. "You said you wanted to stop for now."

"I wanted to wait to have sex. I didn't want you to go away."

"But you're all turned on now."

"What does that have to do with anything? You think just because I'm hard I'm unable to control myself?"

I giggle at his dry tone and let him pull me back down so I'm lying on top of him, more relaxed now like the way we were before we started kissing. "Well, some guys act like they are."

"Then they're either liars or weaklings."

I laugh even more at this, rubbing my face against his shoulder. I'm still aroused, but the momentum has been halted so it's more like a warm buzzing than a torturous compulsion. Maybe he feels the same way.

He starts stroking my hair and back again, slow and tender. "I've waited a long time to hold you like this," he murmurs. "So I'm not ready to let you go yet."

For the next five days, I get together with Theo every single evening.

Sometimes we go out to eat, and sometimes we eat at either his place or mine. On Saturday evening we go to the big local craft fair and then attend a Christmas chorale performed by the town choir. On Sunday, we go to Mass with Tee and Daniela and eat lunch with them afterward. We text throughout the days, and we usually end each evening with an increasingly hot make-out session and cuddle on my couch or his.

But we don't have sex.

And it's getting harder and harder to resist.

I know he feels the same way. He's hard so often around me—sometimes even in completely inappropriate contexts like when we're in public—that I'm honestly not sure how he's managing it. But he's committed to waiting until neither one of us has any doubts about being together.

I don't. I'm even more certain than I was the morning I said goodbye to my pen pal. And pretty soon Theo is going to understand that.

He's got to or I might simply combust from an overload of lust.

On Monday evening, there's a holiday festivity downtown that's held annually called Christmas on Main.

They've closed the central blocks to cars as a lot of the local businesses have put out stalls on the sidewalks and musicians and entertainers have set up stations throughout. The streets are full of people wandering through the attractions, and Theo invites me to join him in making the rounds.

Of course I say yes. I've said yes to everything he's asked me for the past week, and nothing has ever felt better than being able to say yes to him.

I'm not sure exactly how to describe it, but saying yes to him feels like my most natural state.

It's colder tonight than it's been all season, so I'm wearing a long fleece skirt, thick turtleneck sweater that's warm enough to not need a coat, and tall boots. My outfit is as far from formfitting as is possible to be, but Theo says I look beautifully touchable. He seems to mean it.

He's looking quite touchable too in jeans, a dark red sweater, and an old brown leather jacket. He holds my hand as we wander the streets, and it feels like we're a real couple.

Maybe we are.

I thought I might never feel this way again.

We stop by the art gallery display, browsing the works and saying hi to Daniela. As we're chatting, an attractive couple in their thirties walks by, and the man calls out a greeting to Theo.

Theo greets them briefly, and after a mutual Merry Christmas, he turns back toward me.

"Was that Lance Carlyle?" I ask him, watching the backs of the couple as they stroll. The man has wildly curly hair and an impressively fit body. He's grinning down at his wife in a teasing manner, and she gives him a playful glare and a sharp poke in the side.

"Yeah. Why?"

"I don't know. Just Lincoln and Summer Wilson. Lance Carlyle. If you told me you're good friends with brilliant, reclusive Jude Gregory, I'd hardly be surprised."

"Well..."

"Oh my God!"

Theo laughs out loud. "I've only met Jude a couple of times."

"Are you acquainted with all of Green Valley royalty?"

Theo chuckles. "Just to say hi to, and that's only because I'm a member of the country club. I actually know Lance's wife better. Savannah is a cousin to Dan Mills's new wife, Vicky."

I recall the large table at the coffee shop and can visualize the bright, pretty young woman I met. "Oh yeah. I can see the resemblance." My mind makes a connection it takes me a minute to follow through on. "Savannah. Oh wait, she's not Savannah Emerson, is she? The photographer."

"Yes. She's a photographer. She's got a studio in town. She does portraits and weddings and such, I believe."

"She also does some art photography. I've seen some of her pieces in local galleries. She's really fantastic. Wow, I'd never made the connection before. Lance really lucked out, didn't he?"

Theo's eyes rest on my face with a fond, laughing curiosity.

"What?" I ask, suddenly self-conscious at his warm regard.

"Nothing. Just that most people would have claimed that Savannah is the one who lucked out in that marriage."

I shake my head. "That's only because most people prioritize money over everything else. Sure, Lance grew up with ridiculous wealth, but being a rich boy is something that happened to him. Not something he accomplished for himself."

"He's not an empty suit. He's smart and he works hard, and I guess he's highly sought-after as a business consultant. He's done pretty well for himself on his own, I think. I heard he stopped taking any of his family's money several years ago."

"Oh that's good. But still... She's Savannah Emerson. I can only dream of being that good."

"You take beautiful photos too."

"Thank you for saying so," I tell him, leaning over to press a kiss on his right cheek. "But there's a difference. I can take decent photographs, and I can paint decent canvases, and I can do a decent job with all kinds of arts. But I'm not great. I do it because I love it and because it has the potential to make other people happy, but there's a certain level of artistic quality I'm never going to reach."

We've been standing facing each other on the sidewalk next to the gallery as we have this discussion, but it feels like we're in our own small bubble and the rest of the world is a blur of Christmas cheer swirling around us.

He puts his hands on my waist to ease me forward so we're only a few inches apart. It feels like he can see far deeper into my soul than anyone ever has. "Does that bother you?" he asks softly.

I shake my head. "Not really. There's a real pressure that comes with being that good—some sort of creative compulsion that won't always let you rest. I've seen it in Daniela, and I'd rather live without that kind of pressure."

"What do you want then?" Theo asks.

It's the kind of question a lot of people ask, but I can tell Theo really wants to know. It matters to him. So I answer him as honestly as I can. "I... I think I want to feel safe and secure. To be close to the people I love. To make beautiful things and share beautiful thoughts with as many people as want to hear them. To do good in the opportunities that open up to me. And to... to have someone to go through life with."

His hands slide farther toward my back, still holding my waist possessively. His head is tilted down toward mine. "Do you want to start a family?"

"I... don't know. I used to. With Chris. And maybe I still will. But I need to be in... in a different situation before I really want that again."

He nods, hearing me. Understanding. Completely.

I reach up to rub his slightly scratchy jaw with my palm. "What do you want, Theo?"

"I think I want something similar to you. I've never been particularly ambitious for money or power or success. I want to do good in the world. Help the people I can. And I want to feel like part of a community. And I want..." His voice breaks slightly. "And I want someone to go through life with too."

We gaze at each other for a long time, and I think we would have started kissing had someone walking by not jostled me in the back.

I glance behind me, surprised by the abrupt break in the emotional tension between me and Theo. He gently draws me out of the way of the passersby. Then he leans over and picks up a napkin that somehow fell out of my pocket and a small bag that slipped out of my hand as we were talking. He tucks the napkin back into the correct pocket and then takes my second shopping bag out of my hand so he can carry it for me with the first one.

"I think Paige has organized a craft display outside the coffee shop," he says in a different tone after he's collected what I dropped. "You want to check it out?"

9

A FEW HOURS LATER WE'RE KISSING ON MY COUCH.

Really kissing.

He's leaning back, angled diagonally with one of his legs bent up on the middle cushion and the other foot planted on the floor. And I'm sprawled shamelessly on top of him.

He's been hard in his jeans for several minutes now, but he's not pushing us forward toward a particular destination. His hands are moving all over my body, and his tongue is deep in my mouth. He's definitely tense. Just as into our embrace as I am. But it's more like he's reveling in every touch than demanding even more.

I've never known anyone else with that kind of patience.

In truth, I've never been with any man other than Chris. He was my first, and I haven't kissed or had sex with anyone since him. Chris was always gentle, but he also eagerly initiated each next move. He made things happen every time we were together intimately, and I always loved being with him.

But this is different. Entirely new.

The freedom and the power of it is as scary as it is exciting.

He's never articulated it directly, but I know it's true. Theo is always holding himself in check.

Waiting for me.

But he's not frustrated or impatient about it. He's loving this as much as I am. He makes a lot of low, sensual moans as I rub against him, when I caress his skin under his T-shirt.

He took off his jacket and sweater when he got here, and we both took off our shoes. I hiked my skirt up to my hips to free my legs so I can straddle his thighs and get more friction where I need it.

"Theo," I mumble against his mouth, one of my hands tucked under his shirt so I can stroke his chest.

"Mm-hmm." He's cupping my ass with one of his big hands and holding my thigh with the other. I wore thick wool thigh-highs with my boots instead of tights for this exact reason. He's loving the bare skin above the band.

"You're a really good kisser."

He chuckles, his whole body shaking in the most delicious way. "So are you. You're so passionate. You throw your whole self into this, just like you do everything else. I feel like I'm on a high from you. Completely intoxicated. Submerged in all your passion and feeling but somehow not drowning in it."

I've been pressing little kisses against his jaw and neck, but now I lift my head so I can see his face. He's flushed. Sweating slightly. And his eyes are deep and hot.

He's not just giving me a (very effective) line. He means it.

As emotionally affected as I am aroused, I pull off my soft sweater and toss it on the floor. Underneath, I'm wearing nothing but a thin camisole. My frame is long and slender, and my breasts are rounded but not very large. I don't bother with bras much in the winter.

His eyes drop to my chest with a hungry gaze, running over my bare shoulders and the outline of my breasts.

"Okay," he says with a lot of gravel in his voice. "Now I might be drowning."

I giggle until he reaches up to cup my breasts and thumb my peaked nipples through the silky fabric. My breath hitches, and my head falls backward as I arch into his hands.

I let him caress me until my need becomes too urgent. Then I lean forward again in a ravenous kiss. As our tongues slide together, he moves his hands back to my bottom, rubbing it through my panties. His fingers gradually get more presumptuous, but he's still not reaching where I desperately need to be touched.

"Theo," I gasp out. "Please."

He makes a long guttural sound as he slips one hand into my panties so he can stroke my hot, wet arousal. I'm still trying to kiss him, so I make a whining sound into his mouth at the sharp tugs of pleasure when he finds and rubs my clit.

I'm so far gone I could probably come in about twenty seconds, but he doesn't focus only on my clit. He fingers my entrance and pulls my thighs farther apart so that he can slip a finger all the way inside me.

Eventually I no longer have the concentration necessary for the kiss, so I pull away and tuck my face into the crook of his neck as I gasp and whimper. My body is rocking eagerly, like I'm instinctively riding his hand.

Theo is moving with me, making tight thrusts up into my weight as he pumps his finger. He's huffing with our rhythm, occasionally grunting out a gruff sound that might be my name.

I don't care if we're so desperate we're going at it in an adolescent dry hump on the couch. It's still one of the sexiest experiences of my life.

When my rising orgasm coils so intensely that I can't help but make embarrassing sobbing sounds, I smother them by biting down on his shoulder through his T-shirt. Something about the gesture finally breaks all the tension inside me. I come hard, my body shaking and arching through the waves of pleasure as I stifle my loud cry against his shoulder.

He's making groaning sounds as he pushes his finger against the clenching of my inner muscles. He's still rocking up against my weight but slower now, more lingering.

When I've worked through the last of my climax, my body relaxes, and I'm humming pleased and sated into his shirt. He's fallen still too, panting loudly. He's withdrawn his finger, but he's still cupping me intimately with his hand, giving my clit some relieving pressure.

"That was so good," I say when the power of speech has returned. I lift my head to smile down at him. "Thank you so much."

He smiles back endearingly. "You're welcome."

"Now I can do you too."

He chuckles. Looks sheepish. "No need."

"What?" Frowning, I reach between our bodies so I can feel his groin.

He's no longer hard.

I stare at him for a few seconds, processing what it means. Then a little giggle spills out of me. "Did you actually come in your pants?"

"There were extenuating circumstances," he says, still smiling warmly. He can't be too embarrassed. He looks as happy and relaxed as I feel.

"And what were those extenuating circumstances?" I tease him, leaning down to press a soft kiss on his lips.

"Those circumstances were having Maya Alexander coming on top of me. What the hell else can a man do but come too?"

I collapse into more fond laughter, and this time he laughs too, wrapping his arms around me in a hug.

After a few minutes, he does get up and go to the bathroom to clean himself up, and I'm still giggling a little when he returns.

He pulls me into a full body hug as we settle back onto the couch. He gives me a slow, tender kiss that lasts for several minutes.

Then we lie there together, enjoying each other until I actually fall asleep.

◈

Theo must fall asleep too because it's early morning the next day—Christmas Eve day—when I wake up.

I feel warm and cozy but not entirely comfortable. I'm still wearing my thigh-highs and camisole with my skirt bunched up around my hips, and Theo's big body is resting on one of my arms, making it lose circulation.

He's sound asleep, breathing slow and even. I carefully pry my arm out from under him and shake it out to get the blood flowing again.

As I do, I look at him, smiling like a sap at the sight of his thick, rumpled hair and five-o'clock shadow. Even his eyelashes are thick and slightly disarrayed.

I'm not sure how or when it happened, but it did.

I adore this man.

I want a life with him. It might be a miracle that I feel this way again.

After a minute, I'm so overwhelmed with feeling that I need to distract myself. I go to the bathroom and then return to settle back on the couch.

Despite my efforts to not wake him, he blinks a couple of times and peers up at me from under heavy eyelids. His face softens into the sweetest smile, like seeing me on waking makes him happy.

"Good morning," he says, reaching up to touch my cheek with his fingertips.

"Hi." I smile back at him like a dope. "Happy Christmas Eve day."

"Oh yeah. It is Christmas Eve. I don't have to work."

"So what are your plans for your day off?" I stretch out on top of him in my favorite position, pleased when he wraps his arms around me.

"Well, I hadn't thought about it. But lately the only thing I want to do with any free time I have is spend that time with you."

I smile against his neck. "That sounds good to me."

He takes my head in his hand and moves it in a position to kiss me, smiling against my lips as he does. "Uh-oh."

"What?"

"You brushed your teeth."

"So?"

"I haven't. That needs to be remedied." He eases me off him to head to the bathroom. "I'm not going to be the only one with morning breath."

I fall back onto the couch, laughing again. I really can't seem to stop.

Then, since we're both awake and up, it makes sense to have coffee. I make some in my French press as Theo walks around the small space, opening up my blinds and letting the bright winter sunshine in.

We end up back on the couch to drink our coffee, talking about our plans. I always have dinner with Tee and Daniela and then we go to midnight Mass together. Theo's parents are expecting him for dinner, but he asks if it's all right if he comes to Mass with us.

I agree, ridiculously thrilled that he wants to.

It's almost an hour later when we start kissing again. And, not unexpectedly, it gets heavy fast.

Knowing Theo is trying to be good and wait until I'm really ready, I fight the arousal enough to break our embrace and sit up so we can talk.

He's stretched out lengthwise on the couch the way he

always seems to end up. "What's the matter, sweetheart?" he asks thickly.

My heart pulses at the endearment. "Do you want to have sex with me, Theo?"

"Of course I do. You know I do." He hefts himself up to a sitting position beside me.

"When we... when we talked about it before, you said you wanted us to not jump into that until we had time to settle into things. You wanted to make sure I'm ready and that this is really what I want." I swallow hard. "I appreciate that you gave us that time. It's helped me to know for sure that I want to be with you. But I know it now. All the way. You're the man I want, Theo, and I'd like for us to be together in every way."

His face changes. Transforms with an emotion that's awed and full of joy at first but then tightens into something like fear. Or guilt.

Something entirely unexpected.

I make a choked sound at what I see in his expression. "As long... as long as I'm still who you want."

"You're the only person I want, Maya. And it's been that way for a really long time." His features twist in obvious reluctance. "And I want to have sex with you more than anything, but I need to tell you something first."

It still feels like I'm strangling, but I make myself breathe through it. My heart is racing as I resituate myself so I'm not all over him. "Okay. Is something... is something wrong?"

"No. Not exactly. There's just something I haven't told you, and I feel like I need to do it before we... we take this next step." He's not warm and relaxed anymore. He's not radiating that happy affection I've sensed in him for the past week.

He's nervous. Awkward. He's not meeting my eyes.

I try to mentally brace myself as I nod. "Okay. You can tell me."

He clears his throat. "I... I've been into you for a long time. A really long time. I've told you that before, but I didn't give you specifics. I was crazy about you back in school."

This isn't what I expect. I blink a few times. "While I was with Chris?"

"Before that." He's staring down at the floor. His shoulders and jaw are visibly tense. "That... that winter dance your sophomore year. You remember?"

"The one Chris asked me to? That first time we got together?"

"Yes. That dance. I was planning to ask you first."

My stomach is doing weird flip-flops, but this doesn't sound nearly as bad as I feared. "What? Chris wouldn't have asked me if he'd known you—"

"No, no, he didn't know. I didn't tell anyone. I was... It

was my secret. That you were special to me. So that year I finally resolved to do something about it. There was that dance coming up, and I tried over and over again to ask you."

"I don't understand. Why didn't you ask? You never even—"

"I was shy. Painfully shy. And it felt like asking you at last after liking you for so long was an enormous risk. So I was still trying to work up the courage when Chris caught up with me at school one day and told me he'd asked you to the dance. And you'd said yes."

"Oh my God." My chest is actually aching for him. I reach over to squeeze his knee. "I'm so sorry, Theo. I had no idea about any of it, but that must have been so hard for you."

"It was... terrible. I think he noticed you for the first time shortly before he asked you, but he was all in with you pretty quick. And then you two were a pair. Always together. And any hope I'd ever had was... was gone." He's still speaking gruff and stilted. This confession is incredibly hard for him.

"Oh no." I rub his thigh, seeking to comfort him in any way I can. "What did you do?"

He shrugs. "There was nothing to do. I tried to put my feelings aside. Talk myself out of wanting you. But the problem is that the closer you got to Chris, the more I got to know you too. And the more I got to know you, the more there was of you for me to... to want. So I tried to avoid you. Tried not to talk to you too much so I could keep my feelings in check."

"I really thought you hated me and didn't think I was good enough for Chris."

"I'm sorry you thought that, but I didn't know what else to do. I couldn't have those feelings for my best friend's girl. I couldn't let myself get any deeper." He rubs his face with one of his hands. "I tried to be interested in other girls. As you know, I'm not the most outgoing of people, but I forced myself to ask other women out just so I could try to get over you."

"Did it work?"

"To a certain extent. My feelings for you never went away, but they weren't always so urgent and so right in the front of my mind. I really did try. I had a couple of relationships that lasted almost a year. They both fell apart for what felt like natural reasons at the time, but now I wonder if one of the reasons I could never really make it work with someone else is because you were... you were always there first."

I put a hand on my chest. Over my heart. It's aching almost painfully for what Theo must have gone through for so long when I had absolutely no clue.

"I'm so sorry. I was about to say I wish I had known, but

I'm not sure that would have been good. What would I have—"

"No, no. You never could have known. It would have been absolutely wrong to tell you while you were still with Chris. I might not have been able to stop myself from wanting you, but I could at least stop myself from doing that. I loved Chris, and I would never do that to him. I would never be that man. I just... I just held it. Carried you in my heart. But it always had to be a secret."

Something about his words strikes me. Feels familiar. But I'm so overwhelmed with feelings that I can't pin down where I heard them before.

"Thank you for telling me," I say, reaching up to palm his face and turn his head so he's looking at me again.

His mouth twists again. "I'm so sorry, sweetheart, but that's not all I need to tell you." He leans into my hand for just a moment before he eases his head back.

"What else is there?"

With a raspy breath, he gives a brief shake, as if he's trying to wake himself up. "So then Chris died. And... and it was the worst thing that's ever happened to me. But I couldn't even grieve for him without feeling guilty."

"No! No, there's no reason you needed to feel guilty. You never made a single move on me. You never betrayed him. You didn't do anything wrong."

"I hope not, but I still felt so guilty. Because I still

wanted you. So much. I just couldn't make the feelings go away. You were gone then. You left town and didn't come back, but it didn't make it any better. I couldn't date anyone else because suddenly you were right back there at the forefront of my mind when I'd worked so hard to keep you out."

He sounds so anguished I feel like I need to answer the feeling somehow. "Oh Theo. I don't think there's anything wrong with that. You had to work through your grief just like I did, and you had those old feelings to complicate things."

"They weren't old though. They suddenly felt brand-new again, and nothing I could do would get you out of my mind. When you started posting your pictures and thoughts, I... I kept going back to look at every single one. They felt so much like you, and they made me feel close to you in a way I was never allowed."

"I didn't know you followed me."

"Followed you." He breathes out the words like they mean something different. "That's exactly what I did. Follow you. Everywhere you went, I was right there with you in my heart. Until finally... finally..."

He tries, but he can't seem to finish the sentence.

I wrap an arm around him. "It's okay. Just tell me."

"Until finally I sent you a message."

I hear the words but can't immediately process them. "You—"

"Sent you a message. Just some thoughts about one of your posts. Reading and looking at your pictures weren't enough anymore. I needed to... to connect. If I was ever going to get out of my paralysis, I had to at least try. So I sent the message from the account I sometimes use online, and you responded."

My stomach starts sinking as if my body is catching up faster than my mind. "I responded?"

"Yes. And you were so lovely and authentic and deeply reflective—exactly as I've always known you are. So I wrote back, and you responded again. And... and we kept talking. For almost a year."

I slowly pull my arm back. My back stiffens.

Theo is suddenly urgent. Like he's scrambling to hold back an avalanche. "It meant so much to me. Talking to you every day like we did. It... In a real way, it helped me heal from losing Chris. And it felt to me like... like it was helping you too. So I didn't think it was wrong. I kept telling myself it would never be anything but an online correspondence, but maybe both of us needed it. And you'd never have allowed it if you'd known it was me."

I make a weird, choked sound. "So you... you..."

"It was me. Your pen pal. All along. It wasn't supposed to be a lie. It didn't start that way, and then it got so far and so deep I didn't know what to do. Because finally telling you would feel like a betrayal. I knew you'd never liked me, and I was terrified you'd misunderstand my intentions. So I just never told."

It's so much—so overwhelming and disorienting—that I can barely see his urgent face in front of me. I can barely breathe. "So all this time... But you kept... Even now you didn't..."

"I meant to tell you! When you mentioned you were coming back, I decided that this was the time to tell you. That very first day I saw you in the store with your Tee, I came in so I could finally get it said."

"Then why didn't you?" There's almost a sob in my voice, but there's no way to control it.

"I tried. You won't believe me, but I tried so many times to get it out. But I've always been so tongue-tied around you. It's always felt like the weight of the world rested on each interaction because I felt so... so deeply for you. And this was worse than anything. Because I'd fallen in love with you all over again over the past year, and I wasn't sure how I could ever stand losing you."

I hug my arms to my belly. Shake with spasms of emotion.

"I'm so sorry, sweetheart. Please don't cry. When your Tee recruited me into your mystery, I went along with it because it gave me the chance to be with you. And each time I figured I'd finally tell you the truth, but I never did. Then you started to like me. And then you started to want to be with me the way I've always wanted to be with you.

And it felt like all my dreams were finally coming true, but if I told you this one thing, I might blow it. Lose everything I've always wanted." He reaches out like he's going to touch me, but then he pulls his hand back. "But I didn't want to take this last step when... when you still didn't know."

I sit very still for what feels like a long time, staring at his tense body and anxious, emotional face.

He's so upset. Every bit as upset as I am. And he's terrified about my reaction.

And my reaction is... impossible to describe. My whole being is flooded with far too many conflicting feelings, and I'm not sure I'll ever untangle them.

I stand up abruptly.

"Maya, please," he says hoarse and urgent. "Just talk to me. I understand if you're angry or hurt, but we can work through it. I'm sure it feels like a betrayal, but that's the last thing I'd ever want to do with you. I was just... I was just so scared." He takes my face in both his hands, holding it tenderly. "Scared I'd lose everything."

"I... I... don't..." I can't get anything said. I pull out of his hands with a jerk since it feels like the earth is shaking beneath my feet. And I'm falling. Falling. I might never stop falling.

"It's been me the whole time. The real me. I've been my real self with you this whole last year and I've been my real self with you these past two weeks. Everything we shared was real. We're good together. You know that too. We can be... we can be happy together."

His voice keeps breaking, and it's breaking my heart.

I hug my arms tightly to my chest and squeeze my eyes shut through a few silent sobs.

"Please don't cry, Maya. It's going to be all right. Just tell me what you need from me, and I'll give it to you. I'll give you anything." He reaches out for me again, but he stops himself this time.

I can't stand to see his face. See his heart in his eyes. I stare out one of my windows as I manage to force out, "I'd like... I'd like you to leave now."

"No, no, no. Please don't push me away. If we can just talk—"

"I can't talk right now." I sound colder than I feel. Almost brittle. Completely unnatural for the person I've always been. "I need... I need space. I can't even breathe."

"Okay," he rasps as he collects his sweater and his jacket and his shoes from the floor. "Okay. I'll leave for now so you can get some breathing room. But please don't push me away."

I open the door for him, needing to get him away since it feels like I'm going to shatter into pieces at any moment.

He steps out onto my deck in his jeans, T-shirt, and socks. "I should have told you before. I should have been... been braver. I never meant to hurt you, but I can see that's what I've done. But I love you, Maya." I choke on another sob as he continues, "I can wait for you. I can give you all the time you need. I've already waited more than half my life for you. I can wait however much longer you need me to do. But you've been happy with me these past two weeks, and I know—I'm absolutely certain—that we could make each other happy for the rest of our lives."

The final words are almost wistful.

I close the door in his face and burst into tears.

10

I cry on my couch for about an hour, fussed over by two very anxious cats who aren't used to me falling apart like this anymore.

Eventually I run out of energy, so I slump over to lie in a bleak daze for another hour.

The strange thing is I don't know what to feel about this situation. Now that the initial shock is wearing off, I'm definitely hurt by what feels like a betrayal.

But there's also something else. Something far scarier and more bewildering than the fact that Theo kept this secret from me.

It's like the final puzzle piece has been snapped into place, creating a complete picture. And it's that picture—that reality—that has my heart and mind and spirit in such an uproar.

Finally I rouse myself to take a walk, breathing deeply

and doing my best to clear my mind and settle into some sort of peace.

I do feel a little better afterward, but I'm not anywhere close to peace. So I gather the stuff I need for overnight and tomorrow, put the Christmas gifts I've got wrapped and ready in a large shopping bag, and corral Ed and Claude into their crate so I can haul everything over to Tee's.

It will be so late after midnight Mass that it makes sense to spend the night with her and Daniela.

I don't much feel like being alone right now anyway.

~

Daniela is out doing some last-minute Christmas shopping, but Tee helps me unload and then sets us up with tea and cookies while the cats investigate every nook and cranny in the large house to make sure it's exactly the same as it was when they last visited.

To my relief, she doesn't immediately ask what's wrong with me, although it's got to be obvious that I'm an emotional wreck. She bustles around in her normal manner, jumping from topic to topic as she chats and making sure I'm comfortable in my favorite chair and even bringing me a crocheted blanket to wrap around my shoulders since she's sure I must be chilly.

Her familiar kindness makes me cry again despite my best efforts.

"Oh mija," she murmurs, reaching over to pat my arm. "Drink your tea. You'll tell me all about it whenever you're ready."

I do as she suggests and am able to start talking in a few minutes. I spill everything out to her about Theo being my pen pal, occasionally going in circles with the narration and often repeating myself.

Tee doesn't care. She listens to everything with sympathetic dark eyes and wordless murmurs that prove she's following along and that she cares.

When I'm finally done, we both finish our cookies in silence. I feel relieved—less burdened—even though Tee still hasn't responded.

"Well," she says at last. "He is indeed a very shy young man. I can clearly see how it happened. Can't you?"

"Yes, of course I can see how it happened. It was safe for him to start messaging me anonymously, but then the whole thing kind of spiraled out of control. But that doesn't mean it was right for him to not tell me. I get he was scared, but he still should have told me."

"Of course he should have told you. No one could possibly question that. He was scared and made a mistake. So the question is whether that mistake is enough to destroy everything you were building with him."

Something about her choice of words makes me whimper. I fiddle with the handle of my teacup. "I... I don't know."

She peers at me closely. "I've never known you not to lead with your heart. You've always faced every situation with empathy and understanding. Can you really not feel for him enough to forgive?"

"I... I do empathize. I can feel for him so deeply that it makes me cry. What he had to go through for so many years, wanting me but never being able to say so. Never being able to act on it. I have no idea how he... It must have hurt him so much for a really long time. I'm sure I can forgive him. That's not even the main issue. It's... it's..."

Tee waits, but I can't get past the block in my throat. Finally she nods as if she already knows. "I can imagine it might be overwhelming. To realize this new relationship isn't merely two weeks old. You and Theo have been together for almost a year."

"We weren't—" My objection is instinctive, but it's neither true nor necessary.

Tee is right. The fact that Theo is my pen pal means exactly that. That he and I have been slowly building this relationship for the past year. That was the final puzzle piece that snapped into place, and the whole picture it reveals is a fully developed relationship.

"I think..." I take a slow, ragged breath and blow it out. "I think that's what's upset me the most. Starting something new—now, after Chris—has been really hard, and part of how I've been handling it has been reminding myself that we're just getting started. So there's not a lot of pressure. I'm not committing to anything. But now... but now..."

"You thought what you had was a safe little sapling, but now you've discovered the tree has very long roots."

I contort my face to keep from crying again as I nod at her apt description.

"It's planted deep."

"It is. That's exactly it. And of course I was hurt and betrayed by the secret, but I might have done the exact same thing as him if I were in his situation. But now it's... it's real. It's not simply this exciting thing I'm trying out. It's *real*." I reach down to stroke Ed, who is rubbing against my ankles worriedly. I add in a hoarse whisper, "It means I've really moved on all the way from Chris."

When I start shaking again, she gets up and leans over me in a hug. "I'm sorry. I'm so sorry. It's so hard."

I reach up to hold on to her forearms, seeking the comfort I need. "I didn't expect... I thought I'd gotten through the worst of it, so I didn't expect it to hit me this way. But Theo loves me. He *loves* me." I almost choke as I force out the words. "He's loved me for years. And you're right. Because we slowly developed the online relationship, that means we've been together for a lot longer than two weeks. And so maybe I... I..."

"Maybe you love him too."

"He was Chris's best friend!" I burst out, blinded by tears. "And I was Chris's girl. How can we...? What would Chris—"

Tee still has her arms around me like she's trying to hold me together. "Chris loved you, mija. He loved both of you. If he was alive, none of this would have happened, so it's a futile exercise to imagine what he would say now that he's gone. You can only live in the world as it is. And in this world, Chris is gone, but you and your Theo are still here. You've learned who he really is. You've gotten closer. You've fallen in love. And you have a chance to be happy together. It's in that world you need to make your decisions."

My sobs have finally dissipated. I sniff and mop at my face as Tee straightens up and goes back to her own seat.

"How did you leave it with Theo?" she asks after a minute.

"I told him I needed some space to think."

"That was wise. You didn't end things?"

"No! No, I didn't. I wouldn't. Not impulsively. I know from experience my first instinct isn't always the best."

"How was he?"

"He was... devastated."

"He believes he's lost you because he was too afraid to speak."

"Y-yes. I think so."

"Has he? Lost you?"

"I... I don't know."

"Okay. Well, you have time. Think about it. No matter what his feelings are or how long he's had them, you're still free to choose what's best for you. And that may or may not be him."

"I want to choose what's best. I just don't... don't know what that is."

"You will." She smiles at me, warm and knowing. "I promise, you will know soon."

~

Daniela comes home from shopping but has apparently gotten inspired on a project because she goes immediately to the studio and stays there most of the afternoon. So Tee and I spend the rest of the day together, working on some last-minute baking and then preparations for dinner. We still have time for a short nap since we have a long evening.

Dinner is me, Daniela, Tee, and several of her friends—women her age who are either widowed or never married. The food is delicious, and I've recovered emotionally enough to let the pleasant conversation distract me briefly from Theo. Daniela goes back to the studio to work afterward, but the rest of us linger a long time and then move to the living room so we can sit around the Christmas tree as we wait for Mass.

At Mass, I sit in the middle of a pew next to Daniela

and one of Tee's friends, and a few minutes before the service starts something prompts me to glance behind me.

Theo has come in. He sits by himself near the back. He meets my gaze soberly, but he doesn't make any attempt to smile or speak.

He was supposed to come with me, but now everything is different.

"You want me to tell him to go home?" Daniela asks in a stage whisper.

"No! He's fine. He's allowed to be here if he wants."

"You can go sit with him."

I shake my head. "No. I'm not ready for that."

I do my best to keep my focus forward toward the altar throughout the service, but I can't resist a few stray glances. As if he senses it, he shifts his eyes to me each time, and we stare at each other across the distance until I can finally wrench my gaze away.

The Mass itself is lovely and solemn, and it touches me emotionally so deeply that tears start streaming down my face again.

I know Theo will see me crying, but there's nothing I can do to hold them back.

Tee always lingers after the service for a long time, greeting all her friends and acquaintances and wishing everyone a merry Christmas.

So it's after one by the time we're pulling up the driveway to her old house.

The first thing I notice when Daniela's headlights hit the gravel parking area is that there's a car that doesn't belong there.

I recognize it almost immediately.

It's Theo's two-year-old crossover SUV.

"Oh my," Tee says.

My eyes search the dark front yard until they spot Theo sitting on one of the steps that lead up to the front porch. He stands up as we park.

"Oh my," Tee says again.

I get out of the back seat, my heart racing with both nerves and excitement. I walk over to where Theo is waiting.

"I stopped by to leave you a Christmas gift," he says, showing me a small wrapped box in one hand. "I wrote you out a long letter, but then I realized I can't hide anymore. I've been hiding for far too long, never believing I'm allowed to share what's inside me, but I don't want to keep doing that. I need to... to say what I have to say to you face-to-face. If you'll let me." He pauses, his expression deep and hesitant and yearning. "Will you let me?"

I open my mouth, but no sound comes out. I glance back at Tee and Daniela.

"We're heading inside," Daniela says, hiding a smile. "Just pretend we aren't here."

"Yes, yes. We haven't seen a single thing."

The two of them hurry up the porch steps and to the

front door. I hear Tee giggle as she closes the door behind them.

For some reason, the sound of it makes me giggle too.

Theo's eyebrows pull together, but it looks like he's almost smiling now. "Will you please let me say it?" he murmurs. "I'm not expecting an answer from you. You can have all the space you need. I just need to say it."

I nod. Cross my arms over my chest in a protective stance. It feels like my heart might beat all the way out of my chest.

"I ran into Daniela as she was shopping today. I couldn't sit still, so I was walking the downtown streets aimlessly, and I almost ran into her. She asked me what was wrong. I didn't tell her much, but she deduced it was us."

This isn't at all what I expect, so I take a step closer, my curiosity piqued.

"She must have felt sorry for me because she told me about a conversation you two had with Tee about soulmates."

"Oh." I blink. "She told you that?"

"Yes. I've always imagined my heart with a piece missing. A piece that belongs to you. But since soulmates are a no-go, I had to revisualize it." He hands me the small gift, wrapped in lovely red damask paper.

I gulp, my eyes moving between the box and his face. "You want me to open it now?"

"Yes, if you don't mind. Daniela helped me with it."

"Is that what she was working on all afternoon?"

"Yes." He takes a shuddering breath. "Please open it."

I carefully undo the paper and lift the lid. Inside is a necklace. A pendant on a lovely gold chain. The pendant itself is intricately sculpted. Two deep red hearts wrapped around each other.

I gasp. "It's beautiful."

"It comes apart."

"What?" Intrigued, I set the box and paper down on the porch so I can get my fingers on the pendant. As he said, the two hearts can be separated. They aren't hard metal or stone. I have no idea what they're made of, but they're malleable. They bend and reshape themselves into two separate hearts, both still attached to the chain.

Damn it. I start crying again.

He reaches out like he wants to comfort me but then stops himself. It looks like he's shaking with the effort to hold himself back. "I know I messed up. I wasn't brave enough to speak when I should have. I've spent all my life holding back, so it felt like it would crack the foundation of my world to finally speak my whole heart to you. And the way it's happened, maybe I was right about that, but it doesn't matter. I still should have told you the truth and let you decide what you want. So this is the truth." He clears his throat. Drops his eyes before he wrenches them back up. "My heart... my heart was made to shape itself around yours. And even if you can never forgive me, never trust me again, it's always going to be shaped like you."

I'm shaking. Swiping tears away. "Theo."

"And I know you need space, so after this I'm really going to leave you alone. But I wanted you to know that I'm going to do better. I'm going to *be* better. I'm not going to keep holding back because I'm afraid it's not safe. It doesn't matter if it's safe. You deserve everything from me, and that's what you're going to get. If... If... If you want it."

"Theo," I say again, more a gurgle than a word. I look back down at the necklace in my hands, and it's exactly as Tee said it would be.

I know—I know with absolute certainty—what I want to do.

I gently fit the two hearts on the chain back together so that they're wrapped around each other.

Theo makes a gruff sound in his throat as he watches me.

"Will you put it on me please?" I ask him.

He's breathing loud and fast as he steps over, takes the necklace from my hand, and moves behind me. I pull my hair out of the way as he carefully fastens the clasp.

I turn around to face him.

He's staring down at me in the porch light, hope and excitement and a heart-wrenching question in his eyes.

"I love you too, Theo Humphrey."

With a strangled exclamation, he pulls me into a tight

hug. I wrap my arms around his waist and squeeze him just as tightly as he's holding me.

"I love you, Maya," he mumbles, his face buried in my hair. "I've loved you for so long. I can't believe I was so afraid of ruining it that that's exactly what I almost did."

"You didn't. I was just... afraid."

"I know." He pulls back, his face transformed. "We can still go slow. As slow as you want. Just because I made this thing really deep and serious all at once doesn't mean there's pressure for you to reciprocate. It's okay if you're not ready—"

"I am ready. I'm ready for everything." It's absolutely ridiculous, but I'm having to wipe away even more tears. "Not... I mean, not everything, but definitely for a real relationship. With you. That's what I want."

"That's what I want too." He cups my face in one of his hands. "This is my Christmas miracle."

I giggle and burrow against him again. "It's my Christmas miracle too."

~

When we finally go inside the house together, we're too relieved, giddy, and exhausted to do much of anything but collapse on the couch. We chat with Tee and Daniela for a few minutes, but then they head to bed since it's almost two in the morning.

Theo and I cuddle on the couch, too tired to do much talking. Eventually I lead him up to my bedroom. We don't have sex. Neither one of us has enough energy for that. But we get under the covers and hold each other until we go to sleep.

It's Christmas morning when I wake up. It's just after eight and the sun is shining through the window since I didn't have sense enough to pull the curtains closed last night.

I lift my head and see that Theo is still sound asleep beside me.

It was only yesterday—yesterday—that I woke up before Theo and watched him sleeping, coming to the conclusion that he was the man I want.

I didn't know everything then, but the conclusion I came to was the right one. Now it all feels fuller, deeper, realer, heavier.

With strong enough roots to withstand any storm.

He makes a mumbling sound as he blinks a few times until his blue eyes focus on my face. "Good morning. I love you."

My heart melts. "Good morning. Merry Christmas."

"Oh yeah." His smile widens. "It's a very good Christmas." He pauses as he peers at me. "Isn't it?"

I giggle and hug him. "Yes. It's a very good Christmas this year. I love you too."

He hugs me back. Then he starts to kiss me. I'm happy for a few kisses, but then I have to call for a break so I can run to the bathroom to pee, wash up, and brush my teeth. He's chuckling when I come running back to bed, but he won't let me tackle him.

Not until he makes a visit to the bathroom too.

"Now," I say, grinning as he climbs back into bed beside me. "We're ready at last."

He stretches out and gazes up at me from his pillow. "Are we?" he asks very gently.

"We are."

I confirm the words by climbing on top of him and leaning down into a kiss.

This time nothing interrupts or comes between us. We kiss for a long time, as thorough and patient and leisurely as Theo has always kissed me. I know he's getting into it. He's hard in his boxers almost immediately, and he makes a lot of throaty moans into my mouth. But he doesn't rush us. He takes his time, caresses me all over until the kiss and the touches and the deep feeling between us all combine to build my arousal up to an overwhelming extent.

Eventually I can't keep quiet. I'm making greedy sounds as my mouth works against his and our tongues slide together. My hips are making the same rocking motion as his, and soon it feels like I'm going to come from nothing more than this.

"Theo," I mumble, barely able to pull my lips away from his.

"Yes, sweetheart."

"Can we please have sex now?"

"That sounds good to me."

"Really?" I lift my head to check his face.

He's smiling up at me endearingly. "Of course, yes. Are you really surprised?"

"It just seems to have taken a long time."

"Well, maybe we needed a long time." He holds my face in both hands. "But we're here now. Together. And I want to make love to you more than anything."

The old-fashioned term should have felt cheesy, but it doesn't. It feels nakedly authentic.

Because what we're acting on now is love.

I kiss him again and at the same time reach down to his groin so I can slip a hand under his waistband and stroke his erection.

He grunts at my touch, his hips bucking slightly. Then by mutual accord we quickly strip off our clothes so that I can straddle his hips and sink down onto his erection.

I've been on birth control for years to regulate my period, so we don't need to worry about that. My body stretches to accommodate his size, and we're both panting as we adjust to the penetration.

He's smiling up at me, sweating and breathless and adoring me with his eyes.

I'm smiling too as my hair falls forward past my shoulders and I brace myself on his shoulders. Then I start to ride him. He holds my hips as I bounce over him eagerly, letting go of any stray inhibitions so I can take exactly what my body needs.

It doesn't take long until I'm coming with cries of pleasure that I muffle with my hand so I'm not too loud in the quiet house.

He tries to hold out, but it's a losing battle. With a strangled exclamation, he makes several clumsy thrusts up into me as he works through his own climax.

We're both panting and laughing as I fall down on top of him afterward, and he wraps me in his arms.

"That wasn't an entirely impressive performance on my part," Theo says, sounding warm and dry and exactly like himself.

"Well, I came even sooner than you. And it was perfect," I tell him, pressing kisses on his neck and jaw. "I loved it."

"I did too," he admits. "This moment is probably the pinnacle of my entire life up until now. But give me a little time to recover and I think we can do better."

"I'm not worried. We have plenty of time."

We snuggle together for a while, talking and kissing

occasionally. But then Theo does indeed recover. I feel him growing hard against me again.

Smiling, I reach down and take him in one of my hands. "Are you always going to have me be on top?"

"Only if you want it that way," he tells me. "You seem to like to make things happen."

"I do," I admit. "I just get so excited. But I like different things at different times. So we can try it with you on top too, if you want."

He rolls me over onto my back with him on top of me. He grins down at me, hot and possessive. "I like different things at different times too."

We work together to fit his erection inside me again, and I wrap my legs around his back. He thrusts slowly at first as we synchronize our motion, but soon he's going at it hard and fast. I come and then come again before he finally falls out of rhythm, rasping out how much he loves me and how much he needs me and how he'll never leave me just before he comes inside me.

I'm hot and messy and perfectly sated when his hips stop rocking. He's been holding himself up on his forearms, but he lowers his face enough to kiss me softly. "I love you, Maya Alexander. I think I always have."

I smile against his lips. "Well, I haven't, but that doesn't matter anymore. Because I love you now."

He's smiles back, and then he can't seem to stop smiling as he rolls us over to our sides so he can wrap his arms around me. He always wants to hold me as close as possible.

Tee was right. She almost always is.

My heart isn't made of cold, hard marble, fashioned in only one unchangeable shape. It's soft and resilient and human.

So now my heart—my life—can reshape itself around Theo's in the same way his has always been shaped around me.

EPILOGUE

Almost a year later, I'm pulling my tiny house into the Green Valley campground again.

It's always a hassle when I first reach a destination. I have to check-in. Maneuver into the designated spot. Secure my house. Unhitch it from my truck. Unfold the deck. Connect power and water. Unshutter the windows and get everything into livable shape inside. Then let Ed and Claude out of the crates they travel in.

It's not a short process, and today I'm in a rush the whole time.

I haven't seen Theo in almost a month.

We text throughout the day and talk on the phone at least twice a day. But it's not the same. I miss him.

I've had to adapt my travel routine this year so I'm not away from Green Valley for more than a month at a time. I don't want to give up that portion of my life completely, and the travel is a significant feature of my identity as an influencer. I don't want to lose everything I've built, even though I've started adapting my posts so I can continue with interesting content even when I'm in town.

So this is the second month of travel I've spent this year, and this one was harder than the first.

Harder to be separated from Theo.

I've arrived this evening two hours earlier than I expected, so I'm hoping to surprise him by showing up at his place. So the normal chores and routines of setting my house up are more frustrating than usual.

I've put down water for the cats and am gathering the stuff I need when I hear a car door shut outside.

I peek out the glass pane of my front door to see Theo's SUV. Then Theo himself, taking both the steps up to the deck at one time.

I swing open the door just before he's ready to knock on it.

"What are you doing here so early?" I demand, astonished and delighted all at once.

"What kind of greeting is that?" He's grinning as he steps inside and then grabs me in a tight hug. "Finally," he mutters. "I've been waiting forever to do this."

I'm smiling sappily with my face pressed against his sweater-clad shoulder. "It's just been a month."

"Just a month. It was the longest month in the history

of the world." He pulls back just enough to peer down at my face. His hands have settled on my hips.

"I know. It felt really long for me too. But how did you know to get here so early?"

"I didn't. I was just impatient, so I figured I'd come over and wait for you here, but then there were you."

"I wanted to surprise you."

"And I surprised you instead."

I beam up at him. "You always do."

Either the words or the expression earn me a kiss. A good one. Long and slow and deep and delicious.

I get so excited I'm in the process of moving us toward the couch when Claude lets out an indignant, extended yowl at the great offense of being so rudely ignored by his second-favorite human.

We break apart, both laughing, and Theo crouches down to greet both cats and give them their appropriate adoration while I grab the bag he was carrying with him and haul it toward the window seat where he normally puts it.

He grabs it from me before I settle it in place.

"What was that for?" I ask with a frown.

"Maybe there are things in that bag that aren't for you to see."

"Ooh." Intrigued, I try to slip past him so I can investigate this new mystery.

He stops me. Of course he does. He gets his arms back

around me and holds me in place, shaking his head in mock disapproval. "No peeking."

"But I want to peek!" I try and fail to free myself from his grip.

He drags me over to the couch and pulls me onto his lap. "No peeking."

I huff but only sustain the resistance for a minute. I do want to know what kind of Christmas gifts he has in that bag for me, but I wouldn't actually defy his desire to keep it a surprise.

When I've settled and rearranged so I'm more comfortable, I lean against him. "I guess I can wait."

"It will be worth the wait. I promise."

This makes me giggle for some reason. Then I think about all the years that Theo waited for me, and my heart overflows. I wrap myself around him and kiss him again.

This time Claude and Ed don't interrupt us. We kiss with increasing urgency until I'm pulsing with arousal and I can feel a familiar, hard bulge at the front of Theo's trousers.

"Should we go to bed?" I ask against his lips.

"No time for that." He's already hiking up my skirt and moving my legs so that I'm straddling him. "When I said I was impatient, I meant *impatient*."

Giggling, I pull my underwear out of the way while he fumbles to unfasten his pants. As soon as he's freed his erection, I move myself into position and groan hoarsely as I lower myself over him until he's all the way inside me.

I tilt my head down to kiss him again as we rock our hips together in tight little pumps. His erection feels full and tight and so good—filling me completely—and I start whimpering into the kiss as the pleasure coils tight.

Soon it's too intense to focus on kissing. I turn my head and huff out soft, high-pitched sounds in time with my accelerated rhythm.

He leans back, holding my hips tightly so I don't get so enthusiastic I cause him to slip out. He's gazing at me with hot, naked adoration, grunting every time he thrusts up into my bouncing.

He's never been a talker—in bed or out of it—but as he nears climax he starts rasping, "Love you, Maya. Love you, love you."

I come with the absolute certainty that he means it. He means it so deeply. He'll mean it for the rest of our lives. I shake through my release, and he falls out of rhythm right after me, jerking up a few last times until he lets out a loud, satisfied sound and releases inside me.

I slump over him, and he gathers me in his arms again, mumbling again, "I love you."

"I love you too. So, so much."

We hug each other until the wetness between my legs becomes too uncomfortable. Then I untangle myself from his body and go to the bathroom to clean up.

When I return, he's standing up, having a private conversation with Ed about how he understands the neediness, but priorities have to be followed, and Ed will get petted again soon.

I'm giggling as Theo disappears into the bathroom.

I check the couch, pleased I spread out a throw blanket earlier. We have sex on the couch a lot, and it sometimes gets messy. No reason to mess up my couch, which was specially designed to fit into this space.

I've bundled up the blanket to wash when I remember the surprise in Theo's bag. I'm standing over the window seat when he comes out of the bathroom.

"Hey, hey, hey! I said no peeking." He strides over and drags me away.

I haven't actually opened the bag. "But I want to know what it is!"

"Fine. I was going to wait until tomorrow and give it to you on Christmas Eve, but I'll do it now if you insist." He leans over to pull a small, wrapped box out of the bag.

It reminds me of the box he gave me last year with the beautiful necklace I still wear every single day. I resist the urge to snatch for it. "If you want to wait, that's okay. I don't want to mess up your plans."

"I didn't have big plans. I just thought that would be a good time to give it to you. But now is good too." He clears his throat. "Just as well to do it now."

"Why is it just as well?" I peer at his face, trying to figure out why he suddenly looks slightly stiff.

Nervous.

Shy.

I recognize the signs now when I never did until this past year.

He's almost never shy with me anymore—now that he's secure in our relationship—so my heart starts racing in response.

"What is it?" I ask softly.

"Open it."

I do.

When I've undone the paper and lifted off the lid, I gasp and freeze, staring down at the most beautiful ring, gold delicately wrapping a large central diamond. It looks almost like my pendant. He must have had it designed special. For me.

He reaches to pick up the ring, and then he lowers himself to one knee in front of me, gazing up at me with his heart in his eyes. "Will you marry me, Maya Alexander, so our hearts can keep shaping themselves around each other for the rest of our lives?"

I make a choked sound. Then nod urgently. Then finally burst out, "Yes! Yes, I'll marry you, Theo Humphrey!"

There's no use asking me. I have no idea why I use his first and last name.

His expression shatters for a moment. Then he's grinning as he stands up to pull me back into a hug.

It's a minute before we can separate so he can slide the ring on my finger.

It fits perfect. It *is* perfect.

I burst into tears.

Theo is concerned for a minute until I explain it's because I'm so happy. "I never... I never thought I could be this happy again."

His face softens. "And I never thought I could be this happy... at all."

So we end up on the couch again, this time just to cuddle. We admire the ring and talk about when we want to get married and start to make plans for further out than the next six months.

Theo has already arranged things at work so he can travel with me this spring for a month. And he offers to give up his apartment and move in with me, Claude, and Ed full time after we get back to Green Valley.

"I don't have that much stuff anyway," he says.

I giggle and rub my cheek against his shoulder. "That would work for a while, if you really want to do it. But it might be a better idea for you to keep your apartment, just so we have some extra room. After all, it may..."

"It may what?" He angles his head down so he can see my face.

"There may be more of us eventually. And any more

than you, me, Ed, and Claude in here would get unmanageable."

He squeezes me tightly. "Right. Good point. I'll keep my apartment. Anytime you're ready for there to be more than the four of us, just say the word. I didn't think I could get any happier than I am right now, but maybe there's no limit after all."

"Maybe not. Maybe it's another one of those mysteries."

"Well, we have the rest of our lives to solve that one."

ABOUT NOELLE ADAMS

Noelle handwrote her first romance novel in a spiral-bound notebook when she was twelve, and she hasn't stopped writing since. She has lived in eight different states and currently resides in Virginia, where she writes full time, reads any book she can get her hands on, and offers tribute to a very spoiled cocker spaniel.

She loves travel, art, history, and ice cream. After spending far too many years of her life in graduate school, she has decided to reorient her priorities and focus on writing contemporary romances. For more information, please check out her website: noelle-adams.com.

Made in the USA
Monee, IL
15 December 2024

73714473R00121